THE FIRST
KING OF
ENGLAND

BLOOMSBURY EDUCATION
Bloomsbury Publishing Plc
50 Bedford Square, London, WC1B 3DP, UK

BLOOMSBURY, BLOOMSBURY EDUCATION and the Diana logo are trademarks of
Bloomsbury Publishing Plc

First published in 2018 by Bloomsbury Publishing Plc

A catalogue record for this book is available from the British Library

ISBN: PB: 978-1-4729-5174-8; ePDF: 978-1-4729-5176-2; ePub: 978-1-4729-5175-5

Typ~~~~~~~~~~~~~~~~~~~~~~
Printed a~~~~~~~~~~~~~~~~~

All papers u~~~~~~~~~~~~~
from woo~~~~~~~~~~~~~
confo~~~~~~~~~~~~~

To find ou~~~~~~~~~~~~~

THE FIRST KING OF ENGLAND

STUART HILL

BLOOMSBURY EDUCATION

LONDON OXFORD NEW YORK NEW DELHI SYDNEY

Prologue

The king is not a man for action until he's ready for it. I've seen him coolly watch as a boar charges down on him, while he chooses which spear he wants, and then calmly plant himself ready, with the spear butt driven into the ground and him leaning into the shaft, like an old farmer testing the soil with the blade of a hoe.

People have mistaken this calm for stupidity or just a lack of good judgement, and then they've paid for it. Just like the boar that ran itself deep on to the king's waiting spear and then found itself heaved backwards and over on to its side, ready for the killing blow. I've seen the exact same daft look of surprise the wild pig had on the faces of those who hadn't expected such strength, judgement or sheer bravery from the quiet man who watched them closely. But that was when the king was still little known and untested; that was before everyone had heard of the name of Athelstan Cerdinga.

So when the Scots, the Dublin Vikings and the Welsh of Strathclyde made an alliance against the Saxons and declared they would drive us back into the sea, Athelstan merely waited. And then when this alliance of enemies gathered an army bigger than any that had been seen since the time of the Romans, Athelstan still waited.

And even when they ignored half a millennium of Saxon history and closed their eyes to the many generations born on British soil, and said they would cleanse the land of all Saxons and all Saxon culture, Athelstan went on waiting... and carefully laid his plans.

I

My name is Edwin and I am the fifth son of seven children born to my dad, Edmund the shoemaker, and my mother Cwen. By the time I was old enough to work properly there wasn't enough for me to do in the family business. Two of my older brothers were already being trained as shoemakers and Dad said there was no need for another. So I was sent off to find a job wherever I could.

I've been here in the Royal Hall of Tamworth, the chief town in the kingdom of Mercia, for nearly three months now. One of my brothers mucks out pigs for a farmer, and another carries stinking skins from the slaughterhouse to the tanners to be made into leather. I'm lucky. I may work in the kitchens as a drudge, someone who does all the dirty and boring jobs. But at least it's warm and dry most of the time and I get enough to eat.

I start my day before the sun rises and finish long after it goes down. In fact I work for as long as anyone wants feeding; which in a royal hall with hundreds of servants and soldiers, as well as dozens of visiting lords, is most of the day. I sleep when I can. Even so, I still know I'm lucky.

The hall is the home of Lord Ethelred and Lady Aethelflaed, the rulers of Mercia. And it's the place where they train some of the soldiers we need to fight off the Vikings. Mercia shares a border with the lands the Danish pirates have stolen from the Saxon people, and there are constant raids and battles.

I don't often see the rulers of this land; in fact Lord Ethelred is ill in some way and is confined to his bed, so we're governed by the Lady Aethelflaed, and she's far too important to spend much time in the kitchens. If she does venture down here, she just hurries through, taking a short cut to the training grounds where her nephew, Athelstan, son of the king of Wessex, is learning to be a fighter like all royal 'aethlings', or princes. They say he's the same age as me, about fourteen I think, but I've only seen him once and couldn't pick him out from all the other young lords and aristocrats who are here to be trained by Aethelflaed. She's the daughter of Alfred the Great, who first beat the Vikings in battle, and is a great warrior herself. But none of that has anything to do with me. I'm just a drudge cleaning away the rubbish that every kitchen makes; I wash pots and pans, and do whatever the cooks tell me to do.

That's what I'm doing now; the head cook wants a side of bacon from the stores. She has a temper like a sow with piglets to protect, so I hurry off through the smoke and steam that always billows around the kitchens to fetch it.

There are some people ahead of me, but one boy, dressed in homespun like the rest of us servants, is just standing there, slowing me down.

"Get out the way!" I shout at the boy, adding a filthy phrase I've just learned from one of the porters. I don't know what it means, but it sounds nasty.

The boy looks at me and says nothing, but obviously he understands what I've just said because his eyes widen and he punches me on the nose, drawing blood. I shake my head, feeling a huge anger boiling up inside me. Who does he think he is? He's just a servant like the rest of us. And I punch him back as hard as I can, making his nose bleed in turn. He seems surprised, but it's only when the woman standing behind him laughs that I realise she is the Lady Aethelflaed, and the boy I've just hit is with her.

Immediately I drop to my knees expecting to be thrashed to death. I'm going to lose everything! My place in the kitchens, my freedom, perhaps even my life! And as always happens at times like these, times of stress and importance, I see a shadowy black figure standing half hidden by the steam and smoke of the kitchens, watching me. All my brothers and sisters know of her; we call her the 'family ghost' but we know her real name and we know who she is… or was. But now the Lady Aethelflaed laughs again and I tear my eyes away from the shadow.

"Well, that's a punch for a punch, Athelstan, and as you're both bleeding I guess that makes you blood brothers."

ATHELSTAN! The prince of Wessex! Now I know I'm going to die! I've just punched royalty! I risk a quick glance upwards, and see the boy looking at me and the Lady Aethelflaed, his aunt, still smiling behind him.

"What's your name?" the boy asks.

"Edwin," I answer, and begin to feel a glimmer of hope; he doesn't look angry... After a pause I add, "Sire."

"I need a new body-servant, Aunt," he says without lifting his gaze. "One that's not scared of me like the other idiots. Edwin will do."

"Good," says the Lady Aethelflaed. "Take him to your rooms then, but you'll have to train him – no one else has time."

I'm still kneeling, which is a good job because my head's reeling as though I'm drunk. Could I have heard right? Is this boy giving me a new job? He holds out his hand to me. I grab it and he hauls me up still stunned. Now I take my first really good look at this aethling of the Royal House of Wessex and see he's not unlike me: we're both about the same height and we're both skinny, though as he's a prince I suppose I should say 'slender'. But where he has blond hair and blue eyes, my hair is red and my eyes are green.

"Just call me Athelstan," he says, interrupting my inspection of him. "None of this 'Sire' or 'My Lord' stuff, unless we're at some important feast or function. And *never, ever* call me Stan! All right?"

"All right," I agree. "Athelstan."

He grins then and I grin back, both of us wiping blood and snot across our faces as we do so. My head's still in a spin; I've just punched a prince and seem to have got a new job as a result!

"Go and get cleaned up, the pair of you," the Lady Aethelflaed says. "Oh, and Athelstan, put on one of your decent tunics now you've finished shield practice. We don't want anyone else punching you." Then she sweeps off with her entourage of tough-looking soldiers and young women.

Athelstan turns to me. "This way. We ought to get you some better clothes, too."

He shoots off through the kitchens and I follow, weaving around the tables and work surfaces and all the other obstacles. I forget all about the errand I've been sent on. No one will complain, as I'm the aethling's body-servant now, and soon we're out of the kitchen complex.

We quickly cross the courtyard and enter the ancient Mead Hall of the Tamworth royal buildings. Before me the entrance to the hall opens on to a mix of shadow and firelight. Logs blaze in the fire-pit of the central hearth that stretches almost the whole length of the long building, and torches stud the darkness at regular intervals, showing where the gigantic columns stand that support the mighty crossbeams of the roof.

The war banner of Mercia, the Yellow Wyvern, hangs from a point in the roof and billows slowly in a draft of air high above our heads. My eyes follow the slow movement for a second and I allow the incredible good luck of my sudden promotion to sink in. Only a few minutes ago I was a kitchen boy, one of the lowliest of the palace servants, and now I'm an attendant to the aethling Athelstan. My life has changed in the blink of an eye!

"As my body-servant you'll sleep on a mattress at my door," the prince explains. "You'll be part of my guard, so you'll be weapons-trained. Can you raise a shield and use a sword?"

"I have trained with the fyrd," I answer, naming the armed force that every man between the ages of fourteen and sixty has to take part in.

"Fine, but you'll need more expertise than that. You can join me on the training ground tomorrow."

We've been walking and talking and have already passed the long fire-pit of the central hearth. "I don't have much in the way of arms and armour," I go on. "Only the fyrd's standard-issue shield, helmet and spear."

"That's all right, we'll find something for you."

Athelstan now leads the way on to the raised dais that stands against the end wall and faces down into the main body of the hall. This is where the most important people of Mercia sit during the main meals of the day and during state banquets. Aethelflaed, the Lady of the Mercians, would be there of course, and there'd be others: men and women of the royal household and the 'Witan', or Council of Elders, who advise Aethelflaed and help rule the land.

"This way," Athelstan says, and heads for a small door that's almost hidden by the chairs on the dais. We step through into a smallish room with its own central hearth, where fresh logs are burning brightly as though they've just been replenished. It's well furnished with several chairs with arms, instead of the usual stools or benches, and their seats are even padded with cushions. There are two small windows: one of horn, which allows through a small amount of pearly light, but there's also one that has real glass, and light pours in as though there's nothing to stop it.

I look through this special window out on to a world that seems to swim through a thick greenish light, and when I move my head, the trees I can see beyond the palace precinct flow and waver over the uneven surface of the glass like waterweeds in the strong current of a flowing river. It's beautiful and I turn with a grin to Athelstan, who hasn't noticed my fascination with the glass and has crossed the room to another door.

"Come on, we're nearly there."

I suppose 'there' is my new master's room, and I walk over to join him. The prince quickly pushes open the door and steps inside. It's very like the room we've already been in, except everything is richer and more colourful. I almost gasp aloud at the hangings that cover every wall. They're embroidered with mythical beasts such as dragons and giant wolves and they seem to be made with every colour of the rainbow. I've never seen so many colours in one place, apart from perhaps a summer meadow full of wild flowers! There's also a bed covered with furs in one corner, and the curtain that can be drawn across at night is decorated in all the colours of the sky at sunset. But actually, the best thing in the room is as brown as my homespun tunic; it's the tiniest dog I've ever seen, asleep next to a small hearth.

The rest of the dogs in the palace are all wolfhounds and war-dogs, enormous and fierce and trained to kill, but this little scrapling in front of me looks as though it'd have difficulty killing a mouse. It has a squashed-in nose, a round barrel of a body and tiny little legs that become a blur of speed as it walks, which I see as it leaps to its feet yapping. But recognising Athelstan it exchanges barks for yelps of pleasure and begins to leap about like a fat bumblebee.

In fact that's almost its name, as I find out when Athelstan says, "Bumble, this is Edwin," and taking my hand thrusts it under the tiny dog's nose. "He's our friend."

Bumble sniffs and licks me and then with a sudden skittering of his tiny legs he goes to the bed, where he finds a ball and brings it to me.

"Good. He likes you. That makes things easier."

The dog then drops the ball, gives a ridiculously high-pitched bark, puts his head on his forepaws and sticks his bum up in the air.

"We can't play now, Bumble, we're busy."

But Bumble thinks otherwise and when Athelstan pulls a straw palette from under his bed to explain that's where I'll be sleeping, the tiny dog immediately leaps on to it and attacks the edges of it every time it moves. Soon we're dragging mattress and dog around the room while he leaps from one side to the other with happy barks. He gets more and more excited, making us both laugh, and this only makes the ridiculous little dog even more skittish. After a while we collapse in a heap on to the mattress and Bumble then leaps on us and smothers us in wet doggy licks.

It's now that I begin to realise that Athelstan's an unusual boy, especially for an aethling. Typically a royal youth of his age would be desperate to prove how manly he is, and how ready for the world of war and rule he's being trained to take part in. This would involve lots of strutting about and leading around huge ferocious dogs and being horrible to everyone below him. But Athelstan doesn't seem to care for any of that, judging by how relaxed and friendly he's being with me and by the fact his dog looks like a fat owlet that could fit in his pocket.

I'm even more surprised when he begins to chat away to me like I'm the son of some rich lord instead of a nobody who until a few moments ago worked in the kitchens. In this way I soon learn that he doesn't much like the company of most of the other boys who are living in the palace. The sons of the aristocrats of Mercia and Wessex, they've been sent to Tamworth to be trained as soldiers by the Lady Aethelflaed. This is all good sense of course, as the Danes are a constant threat and most of the boys will grow up to spend their lives fighting to defend their lands. But an army training camp is often a rough and ready sort of place that doesn't expect its trainees to be anything other than tough, brave fighters. Good manners and polite conversation aren't high on its list of things for its boys to learn.

All of which probably explains why Athelstan punched me in the face when I swore at him in the kitchens; he'd been training all morning and he'd had enough of brutality. The fact that he'd reacted by hitting me only went to prove he was a true warrior son of the Royal House of Cerdinga, and also a mixture of many contradictions.

Just then Bumble decides he's bored. He walks across the straw palette I'm sitting on, still listening to the strange boy I now serve, and suddenly pours a torrent of high-pitched barks directly into my ear.

"He says we have to get you a better tunic," Athelstan says with a grin. "Come on, you're about my size, so we should be able to find something among my stuff."

I climb to my feet, trying to come to terms with the fact that I am about to be fitted out with a tunic that has belonged to an aethling; me, a scruffy urchin who is nothing but the youngest son of a shoemaker!

"Give me a hand to push this back," Athelstan says as he grabs the straw palette. The fact that Bumble is still attached to it and gnawing one of the corners doesn't seem to bother him as we push it out of sight under the royal bed.

"We'll go and find Master Goodwin: he looks after all of the state regalia and clothes, so he can do any alterations and adjustments that are needed. He's a bit of an old fusspot, but all right once you get to know him."

I look down at my scruffy homespun tunic and feel a complete lout. I've seen some of these palace chamberlains from a distance and they often seem more snooty than the royalty they serve. I'm not looking forward to this. But I needn't have worried. Master Goodwin is small, round and reminds me very much of Bumble.

"Well, he's about the same size as you, sir," he says to Athelstan as he takes out a measuring stick and makes me stand with my arms outstretched as he fusses about.

We're in a room that's almost overflowing with fine clothes. They hang around the walls or are neatly folded in large chests that seem to occupy the whole floor space.

"There's a blue tunic with matching leggings that has a nice white trim around the hem and sleeves. It's seen better days, but there's lots of good wear in it still. Would that do?" Master Goodwin asks.

"He'll need more than one," Athelstan says. "I don't want the palace thinking I can't afford to dress my servants properly."

"Of course not, sir... the very idea! I'm sure we can find several garments that will answer the need."

I spend so long trying on and taking off clothes that I'm finally getting used to undressing under two pairs of watching eyes. Still, it's worth it. So far I've been given five tunics and sets of leggings, two good pairs of what Master Goodwin calls 'indoor shoes' and a pair of solid boots. I've even been given a cloak and hood! I've never had so many clothes – I almost feel like an aethling myself!

My old homespun tunic is then taken and thrown on to the hearth by Master Goodwin, and as I watch the flames eating up the tattered brown cloth I feel that the last links with my old life as a kitchen boy have been burned away.

I can't even guess what lies ahead for me. Even so, I'm certain beyond any doubt that my life will be better. Not only that, but I know that I'm meant to be here for some reason, because I saw the family ghost, the shadowy figure dressed in black rags half hidden in the smoke of the kitchens, watching closely when I first met Athelstan. She's the spirit of my great-aunt, a fierce woman with great *Scinncraeft*, or magical powers, who followed the old gods the Saxons worshipped before they became Christians. She was also nurse to the Lady Aethelflaed when she was a child. We've realised over the years that only members of our family can see her, and whenever she appears we know that something important is about to happen in our lives.

II

One of the first things my new life shows me is that I need to learn fast. Shortly after we've left Master Goodwin, I'm told I'll be attending Athelstan as his personal servant at a feast in the great Mead Hall tonight. It isn't anything overly important, just one of the monthly gatherings that the Lady Aethelflaed puts on for important citizens of Mercia who deserve to be honoured with an invitation to the palace.

But to say I'm terrified gives no idea of the complete panic I'm in. I was a drudge in the kitchens only hours ago, and now Athelstan expects me to attend him at a royal feast and not make a mess of everything!

My confidence is helped a bit by the fact I'm wearing some of my smart new clothes, but I'm shaking in my new shoes when I step out into the Mead Hall in the evening. I take up my position behind Athelstan's chair at the top table as I've been told to do and look out over the hall. The place has been transformed from the massively empty cavern-like space full of shadows and silence that I walked through this morning.

Everywhere is now crammed with hundreds of people who are sitting at rows of tables and benches that fill the floor. And it's brilliantly lit with torches blazing on every column. There are even candles on the top table where the royals sit. A golden light struggles against curling clouds of smoke that rise up into the rafters, where some of it finds its way out of the vents that have been cut into the roof. It smells different too: of hundreds of people and palace dogs crammed too close together, but also of woodsmoke and of the food that's being prepared nearby and carried into the hall. Food I had been helping to make only this morning!

But it's the noise that hits me most of all. It crashes over the whole space like a mighty storm wave. Down on the lower tables near the main doors, crowds of housecarles and other soldiers sing bawdy songs at the tops of their lungs, while the packs of palace wardogs and hunting hounds run excitedly amongst the tables, barking loudly and occasionally erupting into what look like ferocious fights, but which leave the animals unhurt.

In a space at the side of the hall I also notice there are musicians playing tunes that no one can hear. And all around, crowds of merchants and other important citizens of Mercia scream in each others' faces as they try to make themselves heard over the terrible noise.

I thought the kitchens were a noisy and frantic place, and so they are when the cooks are preparing a state banquet and the place is stuffed with chamberlains and servants all trying to collect the food ready for serving in the hall. But even that chaos of fire and screamed orders is nothing compared to the happy citizens of Mercia determined to have a good time!

I still have no real idea of what I'm expected to do, so I simply stand up straight behind Athelstan's chair and try to look as snooty as the other chamberlains and servants who are rushing around with jugs of beer and wide serving platters of food. I've been told by some of the servants I worked with in the kitchens that here in the Mercian court everything is a bit rough and ready compared with other kingdoms, such as Wessex. There, things are more polished and polite, some of our snootier chamberlains say, but I don't think they're allowing for the fact that we in Mercia live on the frontier with the Danish Vikings; we share a border with their kingdom of Danelaw and are almost constantly at war with the invaders, despite all the treaties that have been signed. You don't worry too much about good manners and fine ceremony when the Vikings could come crashing through the gates at any moment.

"You need to pour my beer," a voice suddenly says, waking me from my thoughts.

"Eh!?"

"My beer... in the tankard," says Athelstan, staring straight ahead.

Well this at least proves there's still *some* ceremony in Mercia, no matter how close to the border we are, if my new master can't manage to pour his own drink.

Athelstan nods his head at a large jug brimming with beer that sits in the middle of the table.

Quickly I pick it up and pour most of it over the surrounding area.

"Thank you," he says and I look to see if he's being sarcastic, but his blank face gives nothing away.

Throughout the meal my new master keeps giving me instructions on what to do and by the end of it I am at least able to present a bowl of washing water for his hands without spilling it everywhere. Though I do wonder why one of the chamberlains couldn't have been assigned to give me instructions before the banquet began. Whatever the reason, I learn fast, I have to... and perhaps I have my answer right there.

The evening wears on through a mountain of different foods and lots of drink. But then I hear dogs barking down at the palace gates. Nothing unusual about that, I suppose, but they come closer, as though they are following someone. Then I hear running feet and I notice that Athelstan is leaning forward in his chair. Suddenly the huge double doors of the Mead Hall burst open and a soldier runs in.

"DANES! THE DANES HAVE CROSSED THE BORDER!" he roars. The noise in the hall gets louder, but Viking raids of this sort aren't unusual and no one really panics, even if they are unhappy about a situation that's been all too common over the years. One or two of the merchants, who I guess have property near the frontier, hurry away, and I must admit I feel more than a little nervous; even if we are used to raids happening, it doesn't mean we can't get killed in them!

The Lady Aethelflaed stands and begins barking orders, and within moments the army's commanders have gathered before the dais. More orders are given and soon I hear the sound of tramping feet as the soldiers gather in the precinct that surrounds the Mead Hall.

Athelstan leaps up and heads for the door. After a moment I hurry to follow, and catch up with him just as he reaches the main entrance. The doorway is already jammed with people all hurrying to get outside to see the army mustering, but when they see who's pushing them, the crowd parts to let Athelstan through and I follow in his wake.

Outside, the area is full of soldiers and more are pouring in. They all stand in rigid rows, shields slung on their backs, steel caps gleaming, spears making a high hedge tipped with razor-sharp steel, set against the night sky. These are the royal housecarles of

Mercia, professional soldiers whose job it is to defend the land from Viking attack.

The air is filled with the scent of polished leather and oiled steel and I stare in wonder at this proof of Saxon power. I can't think of anything that could look more powerful and more... *glorious*, but then a great murmuring rises up from behind the Mead Hall, and suddenly the Lady Aethelflaed appears in full armour, leading a tough-looking war band of fighters, and they seem to fill the entire night with their energy and sense of purpose. On either side of the Lady march two shield maidens, and directly behind her a bearer carries the war banner of Mercia.

Athelstan hurries over to Aethelflaed and after saluting he whispers something in her ear, but she shakes her head.

"Not yet," she says. "A few more months of training and growing and you'll be ready. But stay here for now, wait for news." And with that she sweeps across the precinct to take up her position at the head of the army, where she barks an order and they march off.

Athelstan watches her go, a look of disappointment on his face, then he turns and heads back into the Mead Hall and nods at me to follow.

I fall in behind him, but then I notice a familiar black shadow standing at the edge of the courtyard. The family ghost turns towards me and I watch as a pair of ravens rise up from where they'd been sitting on her shoulders, and hover in the night sky.

III

I lie on my back staring up into the deep maroon darkness of the hearth-lit room. Most of the logs have burned down to glowing embers, though some still flicker with flames, and the rich red of their light is reflected in every smooth surface, from candlesticks and the gold thread in the rich wall hangings, to the polished wood of tables and chairs. Athelstan is sleeping quietly in his huge bed and I'm settled under fine woollen blankets on my palette next to the door.

Bumble has been sharing his company between the prince and me. First he snores on Athelstan's bed with his legs in the air, then he wakes up, waddles over and licks me in greeting before settling down to snore and fart on my palette.

I can't remember ever being so comfortable. In the kitchens I'd managed to find a niche for myself under one of the huge chopping blocks. I kept a piece of sacking there that served as a blanket. I didn't really have anything else apart from my small knife and clothes, so everything folded neatly away out of sight in the morning. But because it was close to the hearths and ovens, and was warm, I had to defend my space every night, especially in the winter. I was used to dropping off to sleep again after a sharp battle for ownership with some other kitchen drudge.

So the first couple of times Bumble wakes me with his doggy kisses I instinctively make a grab for him, but he just thinks I'm playing and starts to leap about. Luckily I'm able to settle him down before he starts barking and wakes Athelstan. I soon learn that his favourite sleeping place is curled up between your neck and shoulder or, failing that, snuggled up to your chest where he fatly snores like a huge bumblebee drifting lazily through a summer garden.

"He must really like you," a voice suddenly says into the darkness. "He never slept with any of the other body-servants I've had."

"Do you mind?" I ask, worried that Athelstan thinks I'm trying to steal his dog.

"Not at all. Bumble's a good judge of character. I must've chosen wisely this time."

"I didn't make too many mistakes at the banquet, then?"

"You made loads, but you'll learn. No one expects a kitchen bumpkin to become a polished chamberlain in less than a day."

I lie silent for a moment as I think about what he's just said. "Is that what I am then... a bumpkin?"

A thing called a pillow hits my head hard as it sails out of the darkness in reply. "The worst sort – a bumpkin who doesn't even know he's a bumpkin!"

The following snort of laughter's just what I need to let me know that I can throw the pillow back. It lands with a satisfying thud, followed by a croak, and then sails back again, this time hitting me full in the face.

Of course Bumble has to join in and soon the air is filled with flying pillows and a small fat dog in hot pursuit. I've never even seen a pillow before – I just rested my head on my arm or my folded-up tunic – but now I'm swinging one as though I've known them all my life. We close in to do proper battle and the room is filled with the sound of heavy blows, grunts of impact and the excited yapping of Bumble as he leaps from bed to bed.

We only stop when Athelstan's pillow falls into the small fire-pit in the middle of the room.

"Oh, bum. That's silk... Aunt Aethelflaed's going to be really annoyed."

Without thinking I dive across the room and drag the pillow out of the flames. "It's all right; it's only a bit scorched. I bet one of the chamberlains will be able to get the marks out with a bit of scrubbing."

Athelstan looks at me. "It's only a pillow, I can get another. My aunt'll moan a bit, but it's not worth risking an injury for."

I shrug, uncertain of what to say. The pillow probably cost more money than I've ever seen in my life; of course it was worth risking an injury for.

"Anyway, it's the middle of the night," Athelstan says at last. "We'd better try and get some more sleep."

I settle back down on my palette and then decide to risk asking the question that's been in the back of my mind since the feast broke up: "Did you ask to go with the Lady Aethelflaed to fight against the Danes tonight?"

Athelstan doesn't answer for a while and I begin to wonder if I've broken one of the unspoken rules about not being too 'familiar'. I have to remember I'm the prince's servant, not his friend. But then he surprises me by replying.

"I'll get to fight them one day, but my aunt thinks I'm not ready yet. She's wrong, but I'll have to be patient. And when I do go on campaign you'll be coming with me. As my body-servant you'll be fighting at my side and you'll also be expected to defend me to the death if needs be. So get some sleep, we're training tomorrow."

News comes in early the next morning of a crushing defeat for the Danish invaders. The Mercian army caught up with them as they struggled back towards the border with all the booty they'd robbed from the local people, and the Lady Aethelflaed led a charge that smashed their shield wall and scattered them.

The victory makes Athelstan keener than ever to be a great warrior and fighter. Which means I have to be just as battle-ready as he is, so I go with him to begin training with his war band just as he promised.

IV

The lists, or training grounds, are laid out just behind the Mead Hall. The largest part of them is made up of a wide circle of flat land that is sanded to soak up any blood and big enough to hold two opposing 'armies' who try to defeat each other in mock battles. Here we are taught how to raise the shield wall, how to use sword, spear and axe, and, as Athelstan says, this is also where we learn to swagger like fighting men.

Though I must admit I don't think he'd swagger if his life depended on it. Athelstan hates any type of bragging and show, which completely goes against the usual attitude of the warrior. Some of the boys we train with are 'as arrogant as emperors', as Athelstan puts it, and he does his best to avoid them. But this is difficult in the lists and I soon learn there's one boy in particular, Edgar Oswaldson, the heir to a small but important estate on the coast of Wessex, who seems to enjoy rubbing Athelstan up the wrong way. I quickly realise he's not very bright; I mean, what sort of small-time aristocrat would be stupid enough to make an enemy of a boy from the ruling family of Cerdinga? But what he lacks in brains, Edgar makes up for in looks. He's as tall as one of the old gods, as beautiful as the dawn of a spring morning and as strong as a dray-horse.

The morning of my first day of training begins recognisably enough. As the 'new boy' and also because I'm only a servant, I'm given the full treatment: I find the inside of my helmet has been smeared with pig dung and the hilt of my sword's sticky with grease. I'm deliberately tripped up twice and spoken to as though I'm an idiot almost every time any of the other boys says anything to me.

It only stops when Athelstan notices what's happening. He's been distracted talking to the training officers, but when he's finished, he sees me scrubbing the inside of my helmet.

"What's wrong, doesn't it fit?" he asks, walking up to me.

"It fits perfectly, it's just a bit tight with all of the pig dung that's been smeared around it."

Athelstan's mouth settles into a thin line and his eyes narrow. Anyone who knows him soon learns that these are signs of his anger, and if they know him really well, they hurry to stop doing whatever it is that's caused it.

He turns to look at the gang of fourteen boys who make up our training party. One or two of them are clever enough to realise Athelstan's not happy, and they do their best to sidle to the back of the group, but the rest look either bored or have stupid smirks on their faces, as though they think they've done something funny.

"This is Edwin, my body-servant," Athelstan says quietly, but so clearly everyone on the training ground hears him. "He may not have ancestors that can be traced back to the old gods, and he may not have enough wealth to pay the Danes' ransom if ever one of his family is taken hostage by them. But he *does* have my friendship and he does know that I will not see anything if he strikes back at any boy who tries to mistreat him. He can use whatever weapon he likes, and if he draws blood I'll personally make sure he's not charged with any crime, no matter how high and mighty a boy might feel he is. Remember, you are only here in Tamworth because of my aunt and uncle's hospitality; if needs be I can ask for that hospitality to be withdrawn."

The silence is so complete I can hear the palace dogs squabbling over a bone in the Mead Hall, and it's only when the housecarles who'll be training us begin to shout orders to start the session that I hear the snort of contempt. I'm sure Athelstan hears it too, but he obviously decides to ignore Edgar Oswaldson, who's innocently settling his sword belt as we walk by.

Soon after this we raise the shield wall and there's no time to think of anything but trying to hold our line as the housecarle trainers do their best to break it. As this is the first time I've trained with Athelstan I'm determined not to make a fool of myself, and I settle my shield firmly against his. The order is given and we watch as our instructors march against us in a solid wall of tough, experienced warriors.

With a shout, the entire wall then rises up and roars down towards us like a landslide. They hit us at a dead run and a huge, dull 'CRUNCH!' echoes around the training ground. My head spins at the impact and our line is immediately forced back. I've never known training to be as tough as this. It's impossible to hold the housecarles, but then I dig my feet into the earth and try to push back. I see Athelstan and the other boys doing the same and all the time the air is filled with the sound of the blunted spears, swords and axes of the instructors raining down on our line. I get a stinging blow on my ear, but strike back with my bladeless axe handle and laugh aloud to hear the clang it makes on the housecarle's steel cap.

We've stopped the 'enemy' in their tracks now, and it becomes a pushing competition as one shield wall tries to breach the other. My world is filled with dust, shouting, the dull thumping of weapons on our wooden shields and the smell of sweat. But then a roar goes up. The experience and weight of the instructors wins the day and they smash through our defences.

Even so, I'm pleased to see that I'm not the weakest link in our line, and in fact it's at the other end of the wall that the breach is made, after one of the boys has his arm broken. For the next hour or so we raise the wall again and again until the housecarles are satisfied we won't die in the first Danish charge.

After that it's sword practice and then archery, and again I'm not the worst in either discipline. I'm not the best by any means, but I'm not the disgrace I was afraid I'd be. Athelstan is quietly brilliant in all fields, and when he's set against a boy who's supposed to be the best swordsman, I'm amazed to see how ruthless he can be. The contest lasts just long enough for my master to bloody his opponent's nose, knock him to the ground and quickly disarm him. I then watch as he holds the point of his blade to his opponent's throat and stares long and hard into his eyes with a look of such intense anger that the boy actually begs for mercy.

It's only when the instructor coughs quietly that Athelstan lowers his blade and allows Edgar Oswaldson to collect his sword from where it lies in the dust.

When the session ends, all of us crowd around the well in the corner of the training ground. Buckets stand waiting and we all take turns to draw water and sluice the dust and sweat off ourselves. I notice there's no order of rank here: even Athelstan waits his turn, and no one tries to push me aside either.

It's as I'm in mid-sluice that I hear the horns. They sound loud and long, rising up into the air and telling us that our army is back from fighting the Vikings. All of us boys scramble over to the precinct around the Mead Hall, knowing that's where the soldiers will be heading, and we arrive just in time to see the Lady Aethelflaed riding through the gates at the head of her force. They march with the swagger of victory, and I can clearly hear the cheering from the surrounding streets as they finally stamp to a halt.

Athelstan runs forward to greet his aunt, but I hold back and stay with the other boys, not wanting to push into the family moment. I can see Athelstan asking lots of excited questions and we all strain to hear the answers, but eventually Aethelflaed gives a speech of thanks to her soldiers and dismisses them, then after a short while Athelstan hurries back to join us.

"The messengers only told us the half of it!" he says excitedly. "The Viking army was completely smashed. Aethelflaed herself killed their commander and they even lost their war banner!"

"How many were killed?" one of the boys asks.

"We only lost a few," Athelstan goes on, "and some were wounded, but the Danes lost over half their fighters and the rest we chased back to the border – and even they didn't get away without giving some of their blood in payment for daring to invade us!"

I listen as eagerly as the others, but I can't help noticing the wagons that now start to trundle through the gates. They're carrying the wounded soldiers back from the battle and they bring with them the sounds of agony and fear as the men groan and cry out as the carts jolt along. Then right at the end come other wagons that bring with them no sound at all, which carry figures wrapped in sheets that move only when the wheels jolt over ruts. I notice that some of the sheets are soaked in blood, and others are a strange shape as though parts of what they cover are missing. At the back of the very last wagon, I see a figure in black rags watching me quietly, and above her hover the ravens that give the family ghost her name.

I tear my eyes away from Ara of the Ravens and rejoin the other boys who've now all returned to the training ground and the well. They laugh and talk excitedly about the battle, but I sluice myself with a few more buckets of water and say nothing. The training session is over and when we finally get back to Athelstan's room, I find that a large silver bowl and several jugs of hot water stand waiting.

"You didn't think buckets of well water would be enough to clean us up, did you?" he says when he sees my surprised face. "I'll go first and then it's your turn. We don't want to end up smelling like Bumble, do we?"

"No," I answer uncertainly. And then have to grab the little dog, who is busily trying to drink from one of the jugs.

I'm beginning to realise that I am going to learn something new about this strange boy every moment I spend in his company. The fact that he's one of the cleanest people I'll ever know is just one more piece of knowledge to store away and remember. He not only washes every day, but several *times* a day, and if he gets any mark or stain on his clothing he changes immediately and the article is sent to the laundry. I find myself wondering what he would think about the sheets around the dead soldiers that were so deeply stained with blood, and also how he would react to the figure in black who stood quietly watching as the wagons carried the corpses to their burial.

V

Time passes and I settle into a routine during which I learn how to properly attend an atheling of the Royal House of Cerdinga. Every morning I get Athelstan out of bed, serve his breakfast, train with him in the lists and then wait for him to finish his lessons in the schoolroom with the horribly thin monk who teaches him. In the evenings I stand behind his chair in the Mead Hall while he eats, and then we go back to his room where he teaches me to play chess and draughts.

One night, after Athelstan has beaten me again at draughts, he suddenly asks, "Can you swim, Edwin?"

I look up from the game board. "Swim…? I don't know. I've never tried."

"That means 'no', then," he says. "So you'll have to learn, and quickly. If we're going to join with the naval patrols off the south coast, we can't have you falling overboard and drowning."

"Naval patrols? Where...? Against who?"

"Against the Vikings of course."

"But what help will we be?"

"Probably none at all, but my aunt wants me to gain some experience of fighting at sea now she thinks I'm finally ready for battle, so we're off to Southampton next week. Do you think that'll be enough time for you to learn to swim?"

"I don't know... Is it difficult?"

"I don't know either. We're going to be learning together."

I can't get my breath! The cold water has driven all the air out of my lungs and as I fight to draw in more my throat closes in panic so that I make a loud braying noise like an angry donkey! Athelstan's not much better, but when he sees me struggling he grabs my shoulders and cuffs me round the head.

"Stand up, you idiot: the water only comes up to your chest; you're not drowning!"

I do as I'm told and stand coughing and spluttering while my friend grins at me. "I wish someone would invent clothes you can wear in water. I'm freezing!"

I manage to nod. "Me too... Or perhaps the river could be heated in some way..."

Athelstan looks thoughtful as he shivers uncontrollably. "My tutor tells me that the Romans *did* heat water in huge baths that were big enough to swim in. If only we could do that now."

I nod again, my teeth chattering too loudly to let me speak. But then our swimming instructor starts to shout and bawl and our lesson begins.

Jumping into a freezing-cold river while a crusty old soldier screams extra loudly at you because he can't scream at the atheling he's also teaching is an overrated pastime. I sink like a stone most of the time and swallow river water for the rest.

We go down to the specially dug pool in the bank every day as we learn how to keep afloat and after that how to drive ourselves along. It's a truly awful experience, and to make matters worse, when we get back to Athelstan's room after each lesson he insists we wash, despite the fact we've been wallowing in water for hours already!

When I point this out to him he looks at me sharply. "Fish and all sorts of other creatures do horrible things in rivers. Do you really want to smell of frog fart?"

I'm tempted to answer "yes", but seeing his face I decide against it.

Our lessons continue for the entire morning of every day for a week, by which time Athelstan can swim… in a way… and I can just about keep afloat and move myself about by paddling like a dog. The Lady Aethelflaed decides that this is good enough and we're sent off to Southampton in Wessex to join the fleet of warships that is trying to stop as many of the Danish dragon boats as it can.

I suppose Athelstan as the Aethling of Wessex will be safe enough on board ship; no one will let him drown if they can help it, but I'm not so sure they'll bother too much about me! I'll just have to hope I don't fall overboard. And as for fighting, well, I'm as ready as I'll ever be, I guess. I'm definitely stronger than I was before I started training with Athelstan. All the good food I now get and the fact that I use my muscles every day in the shield wall have made me bigger. I've put on weight and none of it's fat. The same is true of Athelstan. If we meet any Vikings they'd better watch out… perhaps.

We set off for the coast on a bright sunny morning. But for most of the journey I'm too excited to think about fighting or worry about drowning; this will be the first time I'll set eyes on the sea. I'm told it looks like the biggest lake ever, but is in fact much bigger than even that. None of which really helps, because I've never seen a lake either.

We travel fast with a full escort of over twenty mounted soldiers, and Athelstan is riding one of the tallest horses I've ever seen. He tells me it comes from the land of Spain where the Moorish people breed them for speed and to ride into battle. My own little pony looks like a barrel with legs next to this sleek creature, but he surprises me by easily keeping up with the pace, gamely rattling along as his little hooves play a drumbeat on the ground.

It's late in the afternoon and the sun is slowly turning a deep red as it slides towards the horizon when I notice a familiar figure following us. At first it's hard to see as it's so far off, and blending with the trees and the shadows that are gathering on the road behind us, but soon I'm sure that I can see something dressed in black rags and accompanied by two huge ravens. Obviously this journey to war is important enough to attract Ara's attention.

The journey continues and as it's been a dry spring, the roads are firm and mud-free, which means we make good time and arrive in Southampton in less than five days.

We first catch sight of the city as we reach the top of a hill and look down over a sweep of grassland towards the ditches and ramparts of its defences. Athelstan's grandfather, King Alfred, made this important port into one of his 'burghs' or fortified towns that are heavily armed against Viking attack. And it's here that the main fleet of Saxon warships is kept, ready to intercept the Danish dragon boats. It's a formidable-looking place, with high ramparts and deep ditches, but it's nothing compared to the sea that stretches beyond it to the horizon. My jaw drops open.

As I've already said, I've never seen the sea before and despite everyone's best efforts to describe it to me, nothing prepares me for its size and its colour and its smell! It's a beautiful bright day, the sky is blue and the sea takes this colour and deepens it to that of the evening light when the sun has set and the moon hasn't come up yet. I can see fishing boats and merchant ships so far away from the land that they look like toys, and there are flocks of birds sweeping down over its glittering surface.

"It's so calm and smooth," I say to myself, but Athelstan hears me and grins.

"It might look like that from up here, but you won't think so when we're sailing on it. It'll throw you up and down, and whatever's in your stomach will be thrown up too."

I've heard this from others, but can hardly believe it as I stare out over the brilliant ever-moving light of the sea and its bright calm surface.

Then I'm forced to tear my eyes away and follow the rest of the party as they begin to canter down towards Southampton.

We're greeted with huge ceremony, which I suppose is understandable. After all Athelstan is the son of King Edward of Wessex and could be king himself one day. Even so, as we ride through the gates of the city, I'm still surprised to see the streets lined with cheering people. Nothing like this happens in Tamworth.

The next few hours are filled with boring formalities, but finally all of the speeches and feasts of welcome are done with and Athelstan is escorted to his quarters in the local ealdorman's house. I firmly close the door on the last fawning face and lean back against it with a sigh. Athelstan falls backwards on to the bed and lies still, arms spread wide.

"It's hard work being regal, Edwin," he says. "Everyone expects me to look noble and dignified the whole time... It's exhausting."

"Is that what you were doing, being noble and dignified? I thought you had wind," I say with a grin.

Athelstan raises his head and stares at me haughtily. "I'll have you know I've been practising my noble look in the mirror for days."

"Is that right? Perhaps a few more rehearsals are needed."

I watch as he looks about for a pillow to throw, but there aren't any. The ealdorman's bed just has a long roll of cloth to rest your head on. "I miss my room at home already. And I miss Bumble," he says.

"Me too," I say. "But we'll just have to get used to it. Isn't this what royalty does, travel around the country so that everyone can see them and remember they're in charge?"

Athelstan raises his head to look at me again. "Is that how ordinary people really see us?"

I could be on dangerous ground here so choose my words carefully. "Well, yes. But everyone knows you do a lot of other things too."

"Like fighting the Danes, you mean? And being prepared to die to protect the land and our people?"

"Yes," I answer simply and make sure that my face doesn't show what I'm thinking: that many ordinary men, shield maidens and boys also fight against the Danes and die, in the fyrd. But then I feel disloyal for even thinking such things. The king and aethlings and royal ladies like Aethelflaed lead the fighting against our enemies, and without their leadership, Wessex and Mercia would have fallen to Viking attack long ago.

But our conversation ends there as I have to go looking for hot water so that Athelstan can have his night-time wash. I must admit I've got into the habit of washing too, and find it a bit odd that water wasn't ready and waiting when we were shown to the room.

VI

The next day dawns bright and breezy. The group of seven ships we'll be joining, called a 'squadron', will be setting off on its patrol early, so we rush through our breakfast and then we're escorted down to the quayside.

The excitement that people showed yesterday when we arrived in the city seems to have passed and hardly anyone acknowledges us as we go down to the ships. The sun has just risen over the horizon and the sea sparkles like living gold as we arrive at the quayside. Standing out in the harbour are six ships, and the seventh waits for us tied up to the dock. I'm told that our ships are bigger than the dragon boats of the Danes and that they're faster, too. Quite a few Viking raids have been driven off all along the south coast, but I've heard enough of the sailors' talk already to know that the Danes haven't learned proper respect for our fleet yet. Some even think they might not realise that the navy is a permanent force, and they believe each squadron that sails out to intercept them is a chance gathering of a few warships that just happen to be in the area.

But the Danes aren't stupid. I'm sure they know full well that the Saxons of these islands now have an established navy and that one day it will rule the waves.

I watch as Athelstan strides confidently over the gangplank and then leaps down into the ship. I've never been on even a small river boat before, let alone a full-size warship, so I'm nervous, but when the sailors stand respectfully aside to let me follow, I'm determined to look as though I'm an experienced seafarer. It almost works too, but just as I reach the end of the gangplank, I slip and land in a sprawling heap at Athelstan's feet. He grins and helps me up.

"A good omen," he says. "Falling now means you won't fall in battle."

I smile back and try to look as though I'm an experienced fighter too, and that talk about falling in battle doesn't worry me. I don't think anyone is fooled though, judging by the smirks on the faces of the sailors as they begin to cast off and pole the ship away from the dock.

But I'm not too bothered about making a fool of myself. I've just realised something: the sailors stood aside to let me follow immediately after Athelstan, the aethling! I was the second person of our entire party to board the ship. Me, Edwin the shoemaker's son! And now I realise something else: perhaps the world sees me not just as Athelstan's servant, but as his companion, perhaps even as his friend.

The ship noses further out into the water and Athelstan goes to stand in the prow so that he can see ahead beyond the harbour walls. After a moment he turns to see me watching him and beckons for me to stand with him, and when I join him he casually puts his hand on my shoulder.

I smile happily, but then, as our ship joins the rest of the small force and heads out beyond the harbour, I forget everything but my stomach as the deck under my feet heaves upwards and then crashes down with a mighty splashing and spray of seawater. My insides take a little time to catch up with the rest of my body and in fact always seem to be left behind as the ship climbs to the crest of each wave and then slides quickly down the other side.

"A fair day for the hunt," says the commander of the ship who joins us in the prow. He has a mighty beard that blows and swirls in the strengthening wind like a storm cloud before a howling gale.

"Will we see any Vikings today, do you think?" Athelstan asks casually, as though the deck's not leaping around under his feet like a horse that's just been stung by a wasp.

"The coastal lookouts have sent warnings of a sizeable force heading our way. They've counted ten sails at least," the commander says, his legs and hips moving with the roll of the deck so that he isn't staggering about like someone who's drunk a barrel of beer, as I am.

"So we could see some action?" Athelstan asks eagerly.

"There's a good chance of it, though the sea's a big place to lose ten ships in," the commander replies.

I don't hear any more of the conversation because I'm hanging over the side of the ship, puking up my breakfast. In fact I'm so sick it feels like I manage to bring up all the breakfasts I've had over the last week!

The day crawls by slowly and all the while the ship rises up and crashes down and, just for the sake of variety, wallows from side to side so much that at one point my face is dunked into the sea from where I'm still hanging over the side.

I've been so sick I think I must be completely empty now and allow myself to slide back on to the deck where I crouch against the wooden wall of the ship.

Then a shouting voice begins to take hold of my attention, dragging me away from my misery.

"DRAGON BOATS! DRAGON BOATS AHEAD!"

A horn is blown and I hear faint replies from the other ships in our small fleet. Despite the strong wind, oars are raised and fitted and soon the crew is driving our ship over the waves towards the Vikings. Our longboats are bigger and faster than the Danish ships and I stagger to my feet to watch as we sweep down on the dragon boats.

I can see Athelstan in the bow and I hurry to join him. He looks round as I place my hand on his shoulder. "Look, Edwin, the enemy! Now *we'll* get a chance to strike back at them. This is what all our training's been about. We can make a difference at last," he says, his eyes alight with excitement.

I nod and try to look just as excited, but if the truth be known, all I want to do is get the fighting over and done with. If it's got to happen, then let it happen quickly and end quickly too. I'm an ordinary boy from an ordinary background; for most of my life my main aim has been to make sure I get enough to eat to stay alive. But it's different for royals like Athelstan; they learn how to carry a sword almost as soon as they can walk. This is what they're born for, ruling their lands and fighting to keep them free.

I collect my shield from where I'd left it, stuffed under one of the rowing benches, and settle it on my arm. Then I draw the sword that Athelstan gave me. I must be the first one of my family to carry a sword in battle. It's a gentleman's weapon and usually my sort of people carry spears or an axe at best. I try to remember everything I've learned about sword-craft in weapons training. But then I notice a dark figure standing in the stern. The rags of her black clothes fly and wave in the wind and her two ravens hover above her like war banners.

But I haven't time to worry about Ara now; we're closing in on the Viking ships and as we draw nearer I can see that they're sitting in the water, waiting for us. Not only that but all ten of the dragon boats are lashed together making one huge vessel, a sort of sea-going fortress where the Danish soldiers stand ready, their shield wall raised and bristling with spears, swords and axes.

I take my place next to Athelstan, who grins at me excitedly, and I join my shield with his. Soon we're close enough to the dragon boats to hear the Vikings singing. They always sing or chant in battle, and the sound of it reaches us over the water, torn to sound ribbons by the wind.

Now our ship's commander gives an order and immediately archers step forward, their huge war bows already drawn, arrows fitted to the strings. We sweep in closer and now I can see the faces of each Viking warrior. They look as ferocious as I thought they would, but then our ship makes a sharp turn to the left and the archers shoot a deadly wave of arrows as we sweep by. I watch as they tear into the ranks of the enemy and many fall. But then they reply with their own arrows and also a hail of throwing axes. Most smash into our woodwork or rattle loose over the decks. But then I see some of our fighters fall, their screams of agony ringing in my ears as they claw at the arrows or axes that have buried themselves deep in their flesh.

For a while our fleet of seven ships circles the dragon boats as both sides pour a hail of arrows, spears and axes into their enemies. But then a horn sounds from our ship and we turn as the rowers heave in unison on their oars, and with a huge surge we power over the water and drive ourselves into the Vikings' floating fortress.

Our speed is so great that our prow is driven up on to the decks of the dragon boats and I find myself running forward and leaping down on to the enemy ships with Athelstan. He has a bodyguard of ten battle-hardened housecarles with him and we drive like a blade through the ranks of the Vikings, pushing them back and killing as we go. But the Danes are brave and mighty warriors and soon their shield wall straightens and they heave back at us. Athelstan fights like a cornered wolf, but strangely his face looks relaxed and calm as he strikes and thrusts at the enemy before us.

I keep as close to him as I can, defending his right side and allowing my battle-training to take over my body and my mind so that I fight without letting myself see that those I bring down are living people. But I know they would kill me without a second thought if they could, so I strike and strike again at the man before me until I find a way to his throat, and my sword buries itself deep in his flesh.

I step back from the body at my feet. This is the first person I've ever killed, and I almost drop my sword as the shock of it hits me. "What have I done?" I ask aloud.

"Your job!" a voice whispers harshly in my head, and I look up to see the collected shadows of Ara standing over me. "Defend this future king; defend this boy who will make one nation from the kingdoms of many peoples!"

I swallow and just nod, not really understanding what she means. Then the clamour of the battle fills my head again and I lose all sense of time, and my world seems to shrink to the size of the stretch of wooden deck we're fighting on. Athelstan strides forward, drawing us deeper into the battle. I'm amazed at his bravery, and determinedly defend his right side as the enemy rages around us. Suddenly a huge red-bearded warrior bursts into view. He roars like a bear and strikes at all about him with a double-headed axe, our fighters falling like young trees as he hacks at them. He gets closer and closer to our stand, until at last one of our housecarles drives at him with his sword. But the Viking smashes aside his blade and then with a mighty swing he brings down his axe on the housecarle's head. He falls like a demolished wall and now the Viking steps towards Athelstan, who is attacking the line of shields before him and doesn't see his danger.

Without thinking I leap forward with a scream and stand between the axeman and my aethling. With a roar he once more raises his axe high and again Ara's voice fills my head: "Defend this future king!"

I don't hesitate. I rush under the axeman's arms and drive my sword up to the hilt into his stomach. He falls to his knees and doubles over, exposing his neck, and I end his agony with one quick blow.

Athelstan turns, sees what I've done and raises his sword to his brow in thanks, then he returns to the fight and I join him again. I've no more time to think or waste. I must accept my role and defend this aethling of the Royal House of Cerdinga whom I now know is no ordinary boy.

The battle rages on, but at last the Vikings are driven back to raise a circle of shields on the middle dragon boat of their floating fortress. They refuse to surrender, and carry on fighting, but when our ship's commander surrounds them with archers and gives the order to bring down every one of them, they finally see sense and ask for quarter.

They all drop their weapons to the deck and throw aside their shields, apart from two: a man who is obviously their leader and a boy of about mine and Athelstan's age. They stand proudly and refuse to hand over their weapons to anyone other than 'the leader of the Saxons', as the man says. This is the first time I realise Saxon and Dane can understand each other. Their accent is strange, but the words are the same as ours.

I expect our ship's commander to step forward, but instead he turns to Athelstan and bows his head. When Athelstan approaches the Vikings I go with him, sword ready in case of treachery.

He stops before the two Danes and gazes at them unflinchingly. The man stares down at us from what seems like a gigantic height and says, "Who are you, boy, who thinks he has the authority to take the weapons from the hands of Viking warriors?"

Athelstan remains silent for just long enough to make the Danish boy shift uncomfortably and then he says, "I am Athelstan Cerdinga, Aethling of Wessex, and grandson of King Alfred who defeated Guthrum of the Danish Great Army at the Battle of Eddington. Who are you who believes he has the right to question a scion of the greatest royal house on these islands?"

The man smiles and then throws back his head and laughs. "My Lord, I am Swain Ericsson and this is my son Olaf."

"Then surrender your weapons, Swain Ericsson and Olaf Swainson. Your battle is lost and you will now be taken to face our judgement."

The man drops his sword at his feet, but I watch in surprise as the boy steps forward and presents his sword hilt first to my master and friend. On the edge of my sight I'm aware of a dark figure watching, and as Athelstan takes the offered sword I clearly hear the triumphant cry of ravens.

VII

The Lady Aethelflaed is full of praise for Athelstan when we get back to the Royal Hall of Tamworth in Mercia. She even has time to thank me for protecting her nephew so well in the sea battle, and when we're called to stand and present ourselves to the Mead Hall during the victory feast that's been arranged I feel as though I'm going to burst with pride as everyone cheers us, even the veteran housecarles who have their own table near the doors.

Of course I know that really they're just cheering the aethling Athelstan, but I feel I've earned a bit of the praise too and allow myself to grin broadly as the noise rises to the rafters.

The evening passes in its usual blur of eating, drinking and, as the beer and mead takes a stronger hold, lots of singing, ranging from battle paeans to some more 'lusty' ditties involving unlikely physical acts! But at last the celebrations slowly wind down to an exhausted murmuring and Athelstan decides it's all right for us to leave.

As we finally shut the door of Athelstan's room on the night and its revelry, Bumble bustles up, barking and wagging his tail so furiously it's just a blur. The little dog missed us when we were away fighting the Vikings and now he jumps about for a few seconds while I pull my straw palette from under the bed, and then he hurries off to return with a leather ball in his mouth.

"You play with him, I'm too exhausted," Athelstan says, yawning wildly.

I throw the ball listlessly a few times and grin as I suddenly realise that Bumble's as round as the ball he's chasing – the only difference is the fact that one of the round objects has legs.

"He missed us badly when we were away," I say as I throw the ball again. "One of the chamberlains told me he hardly ate anything."

"Well that can't be true," says Athelstan with a snort. "Look at him, he's as fat as butter!"

"I hear that's because the Lady Aethelflaed felt sorry for him and fed him by hand from her own plate."

"She can't have had much to eat herself then. He looks even more like a bumblebee than he did before we set off. All he needs are a couple of wings and a stripy coat."

I grin and nod, but then Athelstan adds, "But perhaps you're right. Next time we go off to fight we'll take him with us."

I look at him in amazement. "But he won't last a day in camp and the Danes will swat him like a fly if they get near him!"

"No problem. I've decided to have him trained as a war-dog. He can defend me in battle."

Of course we all know that war-dogs are huge, ferocious creatures such as mastiffs and wolfhounds, the exact opposite of our tiny, gentle little Bumble. It's such a ridiculous idea that our minuscule mutt could be trained to kill that I begin to laugh, and as Athelstan joins in Bumble bounces around in happy excitement, ready as always for fun.

VIII

The next day we go to see Olaf, the Viking chief's son who we took prisoner after the sea battle. His father paid a huge ransom in gold for his own freedom and that of his men, but had to agree to leave Olaf behind as hostage to ensure he doesn't attack the Wessex coast again.

It can't be comfortable being a hostage. No one can say how long you'll be held, and if your family breaks the agreed terms you'll be executed. Simple and nasty. Olaf is being held in the palace and has his own room, but any door that bolts from the outside and has two housecarles standing guard over it makes even the most comfortable quarters seem a prison.

On the journey back to Mercia, we spent quite a bit of time with Olaf. It was then I realised that it's possible to like the Danes. It helped that our hostage had the same sense of humour as me and could tell some eye-wateringly dirty jokes.

At first Athelstan was a bit wary of him, but eventually even he couldn't help liking the Danish boy's natural friendliness and sense of fun. It took him a while to understand the Danish accent, but I had no difficulties; obviously the languages of the lower-class Danes and Saxons are closer to each other than the languages of the Danes and Saxon royalty.

We arrive at Olaf's door and Athelstan dismisses the guards. They're pretty reluctant to leave him to us, but we point out that we defeated the young Viking in battle and as there are two of us it won't be easy for him to escape.

The housecarles are still doubtful and eventually Athelstan is forced to 'go all royal on them' as he puts it, and orders them to leave. When they've gone we pull back the bolts and open the door. Like I say, the room is quite comfortable, but Olaf's sitting on the bed and for once he seems down.

"Eh up, mate," I say in my best rough Saxon. "You all right?"

He shrugs. "I suppose, but…"

"But what?" I ask.

"When can I go home? When will you think it's safe enough to let me go?"

I look at Athelstan, whose face is screwed up into a scowl of concentration as he slowly works out what the Viking boy is saying. At last his face clears and he shrugs. "I don't know… When we know your dad won't raid the Wessex coast again, I suppose."

"But how can you know that?" Olaf asks. "The only way you could really be certain is if he's dead."

This is true, of course, and Athelstan just shakes his head, unable to offer any answer.

"Let's not worry about things we can't change," I say eventually. "I tell you what, perhaps Athelstan can persuade his aunt to give you a bit more freedom, then maybe you could spend more time with us."

I feel really sorry for him. If the circumstances had been only slightly different, we could've been captured in the battle and held to ransom by Swain, Olaf's dad. I don't suppose anyone would've paid much for me, but Swain could've demanded enough gold for Athelstan to build a fleet of dragon boats.

"I'm not sure Aunt Aethelflaed will let Olaf spend much time with us. He could overhear all sorts of information and pass it on to the Vikings," says Athelstan.

"How? He's a hostage; what's he going to do – write a letter and send it by secret messenger?" I look at the Danish boy sitting on his bed. "I bet he can't even write!"

"I can't," Olaf says. "I had the chance to learn but I was always more interested in ships and fighting… Fat lot of good that did me."

Athelstan goes quiet and stands in thought for a while, then says, "All right, we'll give it a try. We can go to my aunt now and introduce Olaf to her, then she can see he's just a lad like us."

Olaf looks worried. "I'm not sure about meeting the Lady Aethelflaed," he says nervously. "I hear she tortures Danes for fun and always slaughters her prisoners."

"Don't be daft," says Athelstan sharply. "Those are just scare stories made up by you Vikings. She's an honourable woman and a great fighter."

Olaf still looks unconvinced, but before he can say anything Athelstan starts to move and writhe strangely as though he's having a fit.

"Keep still!" he says to his tunic and I start to think he's going mad.

"And stop licking me!" he demands.

"I'm nowhere near you!" I answer.

"Not you," he says. "Him!"

"Me?" Olaf snorts with laughter. "You're six paces away – my tongue's not that long!"

"Not you either… HIM!"

I watch as suddenly he pulls off his tunic and unbuttons his shirt. "What are you doing?" I ask in bewilderment.

"He's going *bare-sark*, like our best warriors," Olaf splutters through his laughter. "When the spirits of battle possess them they rip off their clothes and fight naked."

"I'm not going bare-sark!" says Athelstan, outraged. "It's him, wriggling about!" And he reaches inside his shirt and pulls out Bumble, who barks happily at us all.

"What's he doing inside your tunic?" I ask, totally puzzled.

"Well, you yourself said that he missed us when we were away, so I thought I'd keep him with us as much as possible today, and it just seemed easier to put him in my shirt rather than put him on a lead and wait for him to sniff at every vile smell he comes across."

"Couldn't you have just carried him in your arms?"

"I thought I might need my arms and hands for other things."

I find myself just staring in wonder at the way Athelstan's mind works. Perhaps it's something to do with being royal.

"Yeah fine, so you carried it in your shirt," Olaf interrupts, looking at Bumble as if he's some weird creature from the sagas. "But could you please tell me what exactly it is?"

"He's my dog," Athelstan says simply.

"That's a *dog*?!" Olaf asks in amazement.

Bumble barks as though answering him, and he jumps from his master's arms and waddles over to the young Viking, his tail wagging. Olaf reaches down and picks him up, and immediately gets his face covered in doggy licks.

The boy laughs. "He's great, but I don't think he can be a dog."

"I can assure you he is," says Athelstan.

"But what's he for? Surely he can't hunt anything, not even rats, and he's obviously nobody's idea of a war-dog," says Olaf, a puzzled frown on his face. "What does he do?"

"He makes people feel happy," I say into the silence that follows.

The young Viking stares at Bumble, who has now snuggled down into the crook of his arm and is yawning between making feeble attempts to lick his new friend again. "Yeah... yeah, I can see that. He's certainly made me laugh... and feel better."

"Good," says Athelstan decisively. "We'll take him with us to see Aunt Aethelflaed."

IX

When we get to the Council Chamber where Aethelflaed is, we find she's in conference with several commanders from the Mercian army. When they see Olaf, they all go quiet and stare.

"Why have you brought the hostage here with you?" Aethelflaed asks pointedly.

"He was bored in his room, so we thought we'd let him spend time with us," Athelstan answers.

"But he's a hostage," a harsh voice suddenly says, filling the stone-built chamber with its power. "Hostages aren't supposed to enjoy themselves."

Athelstan stiffens and turns to a figure we hadn't noticed lounging in the chair next to Aethelflaed.

"Dad! When did you get here? Why wasn't I told you were visiting?"

The figure stands and I can't help noticing how alike man and boy are... at least in appearance. "I got here last night and you weren't told because I gave instructions that you shouldn't be."

"Why?"

"Because I'm here to see my sister, not my son. Your aunt Aethelflaed and I are planning a war and you can't contribute anything of any value to that."

I watch as my friend begins to scowl. Obviously there's no love between father and son here. In fact, I doubt there's even any friendship.

"I think we need to keep details to ourselves in the presence of an enemy hostage," the Lady Aethelflaed says, and King Edward of Wessex, Athelstan's father, nods.

"Take away the Danish boy and lock him up," says the king, but Athelstan steps protectively in front of Olaf.

"According to the wording of the treaty signed by the Reeve of Southampton, Olaf Swainson is under the protection and care of the Wessex court until such time as an agreement is reached concerning his release. Nothing was said about him being locked up."

"And what would you know about treaties?" King Edward asks, his harsh voice echoing back from the chamber's high ceiling.

"Of this particular one, a great deal," says Athelstan steadily. "Olaf was taken in the battle I fought against a fleet of raiding dragon boats off the south coast of Wessex, and I made a point of learning as much as possible about all the procedures that follow the capture of enemy goods and personnel. Therefore I know that Olaf Swainson is not only under the protection of the Wessex court, but he's also my personal *guest*, as I was the only member of the ruling House of Cerdinga present when the Danish raiders surrendered."

King Edward looks unblinkingly at his son for what seems like for ever, but then he nods. "I see you're a good scholar, and a good fighter too I hear. Your aunt's training is making a proper Saxon leader of you."

Athelstan nods his head in turn, and I realise I've been holding my breath throughout this. Being in the same room as King Edward feels like standing out in the open during a storm and waiting to be struck by lightning, but after watching the proud way Athelstan handled himself during this... discussion, I now realise he's at least as strong as his dad. What sort of king will he make if the council chooses him to rule Wessex after his dad is dead?

"Well, as Olaf is your *guest,* perhaps you should take him around the artisan quarter," the Lady Aethelflaed says. "I'm sure he'll be interested in the work of the swordsmiths. But Athelstan, be careful you don't go anywhere near places that might provide useful information for any Viking commanders your friend may know."

Athelstan smiles in agreement, but his face settles back into a scowl as he nods politely to his father.

Outside the Council Chamber, Olaf lets out a long sigh of relief. "That was King Edward of Wessex," he almost squeaks. "He's one of the greatest Saxon fighters alive today!"

"Yes, we know. He's my dad," Athelstan points out.

"Oh yeah!" the young Viking says as though he's only just understood this fact. "Of course he is. No wonder you fought so well in the battle."

Athelstan smiles at him and then says, "Come on, this way. My aunt's right. I bet you will be interested in the sword-weavers."

He leads the way through the palace, out into the royal precinct and then through the huge double gates where all the artisans and craftspeople attached to the court have their workshops. The scent of hot metal, smoke and boiling dye vats fills the air as we travel through each of the areas that are dedicated to all the individual arts and crafts.

Now that we're well away from the Council Chamber and King Edward, I at last have the chance to ask the question that's been niggling me: "How did you remember the wording of the treaty about Olaf?" I ask. "You know, the bit about him being a guest and under the protection of the Wessex court?"

"I didn't," Athelstan says with a grin. "I've no idea what's in the treaty, but I guessed my dad doesn't either. I know he won't risk arguing a point if he doesn't know for certain he's right. If you're going to lie, do it with confidence – that way everyone will believe you."

Olaf laughed. "I think we Danes are going to need to watch our borders closely when you become king."

"That's right," Athelstan says seriously. "You are."

We spend a happy few hours wandering around the workshops. The swordsmiths' forges are a nightmare of deep shadows and fiery light and when the smiths beat out the red-hot blades of the new swords on their huge black anvils, sparks fly through the air like tiny comets trailing blazing light across the night sky. Then the entire workshop is filled with a great, roaring, boiling hiss, like a pit full of giant snakes, as the red-hot metal is quenched in vats of water and a rolling cloud of steam brings a warmth filled with the smell of iron.

"How many of those new swords will draw Danish blood?" Olaf asks quietly.

"As many as the blades being made by Viking smiths that will draw Saxon blood," Athelstan answers. "But perhaps... perhaps it doesn't always have to be so..."

"How can it not?" I ask. "Saxons and Danes have been fighting for years. How can there ever be a lasting peace? We Saxons want back the land the Danes have stolen from us, and the Danes want even more land than they already have. Everyone knows that any peace treaty between our two sides is just a pause in the fighting that we'll both use to get ready for the next war. How can there ever be peace between us?"

"I don't know," Athelstan admits. "But when we're not fighting, we trade, and when we trade we talk and we find Danes and Saxons are the same... almost. We have the same needs, the same interests. And we all know there are children in the lands around us that have a mixing of Danish and Saxon blood. So it seems that though we hate each other, we can love each other too."

"That's true, I suppose," I say, and playfully cuff Olaf around the head. "This Viking cub stinks like a Viking, and is as stupid as a Viking, but he's all right, really, I suppose."

"Yeah, you Saxons are nothing like I thought you'd be too. I quite like you in a way," says Olaf, looking us over as though we're a pair of horses he's thinking of buying. "I might not even object too much if you wanted to marry one of my sisters."

"Well, thank you," Athelstan replies seriously. "Perhaps this is a conversation we should all remember when we're older and might be in a position to make something out of the possibility of...well, what...? *Friendship?*"

"Friendship?! I wouldn't go that far," says Olaf. "But perhaps we'll be able to put up with each other and get along when we have to. I have an aunt and uncle like that; they stay together because he's a good earner and she's good at running their lives. And as my aunt says, winters are long and cold and a face looking back at you from the other side of the fire is better than no face at all, even if it does look like a slapped arse."

"Yes," says Athelstan brightly. "That's it precisely."

X

Later that night the Lady Aethelflaed herself comes to Athelstan's room, supposedly to ask how we spent our time in the artisans' quarter. We still have Olaf with us and she makes a point of being nice to him. So much so that the young Viking overcomes his fears and is soon smiling and chatting to her as though he's known her for years. But then she insists we all settle down for the night and she calls a housecarle guard to escort Olaf back to his room.

After he's gone, however, she shows no signs of leaving and instead seats herself more comfortably in one of the padded chairs and then turns to look unwaveringly at her nephew. Even though I'm not the object of her attention I feel like a mouse being closely watched by a powerful cat.

I know something important is about to happen because over by the wall, in the deepest shadows, I can see Ara of the Ravens watching quietly. The black rags she wears stream wildly about her as though she's standing in the middle of a powerful storm, but all is still and quiet in the room.

"Do you think Olaf learned anything from you today, Athelstan?" Aethelflaed asks quietly.

I watch as my young master sits in a chair opposite his aunt and returns her unwavering gaze without flinching. "If you mean, did I reveal the strength of our army, the weak points in our defences and our plans to invade Danelaw – then no, Aunt, Olaf learned nothing."

Aethelflaed laughs. "Oh, you are so like your father."

"Who, incidentally, still hasn't found time to visit his son during his secret mission to Mercia," Athelstan says, without a trace of bitterness in his voice.

"No, I'm afraid we've been very busy," Aethelflaed answers. "And now your father's left. He's on his way back to Wessex to raise the royal army."

"Where will he strike?" Athelstan asks, showing no surprise at the news.

"Northumbria. We're both leading a combined army of Mercia and Wessex against the Danes there."

"Why?"

"Because they need to learn that our Saxon alliance should be treated with respect. There've been too many raids along the Wessex coast and over our border with Danelaw."

"And will I be included in this campaign?" Athelstan asks, and I hear the eagerness in his voice.

"Not this time," Aethelflaed says, and raises her hand to stop his protests before they begin. "But I promise that you will be included in the next campaign, no matter what."

"Then I accept your promise and will hold you to it."

"Would you dare impose terms on the Lady of the Mercians?" his aunt asks sharply.

"As the paramount Aethling of Wessex, yes I would, Aunt Aethleflaed. I most definitely would."

She smiles. "Good. But remember, Athelstan, keep these plans to yourself. No loose talk in front of Olaf. We intend to take the Danes completely by surprise."

She stands then ready to leave, but suddenly I feel her eyes on me. "And that applies to you too, Edwin. I will extract a high price for every morsel of information that might fall from your lips."

"Nothing shall fall from my lips or from any other part of me," I say hurriedly.

"That conjures an unpleasant image," the Lady says, and she heads for the door.

But now I'm distracted as the room is filled with the sound of Ara's ravens calling wildly. Athelstan obviously hears nothing, but Aethelflaed stops and looks back into the room for a moment, before she gives a slight shake of her head and leaves.

Two days later we're riding away from Tamworth and the palace of Mercia. Athelstan's aunt has told us we can go on a hunting trip and that we can take Olaf with us. I personally think she just wants us out of the way so that Athelstan doesn't have to watch another army march off to battle without him. She warns us to go nowhere near the frontier where Mercia meets Danelaw and to stay in the south near the border with Wessex. We agree and set off with an escort of five housecarles, all armed to the teeth and slowing us down as they trudge behind mine and Olaf's ponies and Athelstan's tall Moorish horse.

When we reach a settlement that's big enough to have several taverns, Athelstan bribes the housecarles to spend the next few nights there, drinking and getting to know the local girls, after which we'll meet up with them again and return to Tamworth Palace together. It takes a while to settle negotiations, but when Athelstan has almost emptied his purse of gold coins, the housecarles agree terms and we set off.

"Why did you bribe them to stay here?" I ask. "We could've just ridden off and left them behind if we wanted to."

"I didn't want to get them into trouble with their commanders because they let us get away from them. Besides, I have a plan and I don't want any annoyed housecarles reporting back to Tamworth until it's been carried out."

"What sort of plan?" I ask.

"I'll tell you when I'm ready," he answers.

Olaf and I spend a good part of that first day's journey muttering to each other as we try to work out what the plan could be and where we're going.

"I've already said I'll tell you when I'm ready," Athelstan suddenly snaps, annoyed with our whisperings. "I've got to get my bearings first."

"If you tell us your plan perhaps we can help," Olaf says.

"I don't need any help, just a few landmarks to show me where we are."

"I hope you don't think the Lady Aethelflaed was fooled into thinking we're going hunting," I say. "Anyone with half a thought in their head would know there wasn't any chance of that as soon as they saw we had no spears and no nets with us and, more importantly, that we had no dogs with us either."

Athelstan laughed. "We have our war bows with us. They could easily bring down a deer or even a boar, but you're right, I'm sure my aunt has already guessed exactly where we're going and why. And we do have one dog with us at least."

At this exact moment we hear a barking from one of the large saddlebags slung over the haunches of Athelstan's horse, and Bumble pokes out his head and pants at us, his wide mouth looking exactly like a grin. He's obviously been asleep, snuggled down amongst all our spare clothing and other luggage we've brought with us.

"When did you smuggle him into the baggage?" I ask, amazed to see the little animal.

"Smuggle? *Smuggle!?* An aethling of the Cerdinga doesn't smuggle anything, he merely packs what he wants to bring with him," Athelstan replies haughtily, before spoiling the effect and grinning.

"Well, I'm just surprised you packed anything at all... In fact I'm amazed you knew *how* to pack anything, let alone a squirming little lapdog like Bumble."

"I keep telling you, that's not a dog," Olaf says. "It's a slug that's somehow grown legs."

Bumble barks again and then slowly slips back down into the saddlebag for another snooze.

"Aha!" Athelstan suddenly shouts triumphantly and points at a tree on the skyline that he's obviously only just noticed. "The lightning-struck oak beside the granite outcrop! I know exactly where we are now."

"Can *we* be told then?" I ask.

"Certainly – we're half a day's march from Tamworth, heading east."

"Thanks," I say. "But exactly why are we half a day's march from Tamworth, heading east…" My voice trails away as a thought occurs. "Surely you're not planning to join with King Edward and your aunt on their campaign against the Danes?!"

"Certainly not. I have an agreement with the Lady Aethelflaed. Besides, the army's marching north, while we are going east into Danelaw."

"WHAT?!" I screech. "Danelaw? Why?"

"We're taking Olaf home, or at least we're taking him back to his own people where, hopefully, they'll help him get back to his family."

My reply is interrupted by the sound of Olaf falling off his pony. He's unhurt, but lies on his back with his mouth wide open. Eventually it snaps shut.

"Why?" he asks eventually. "Why are you helping me, a Dane and an enemy?"

Athelstan shrugs from his position high on his tall horse. "Because I like you and being a hostage is a dangerous game. You could be… Well, you could be executed at any time, and I wouldn't like that. I wouldn't like that at all."

I help Olaf back on to his pony, my head spinning. Once again I'm amazed by the boy I serve. Who else in the whole of the Mercian court would've thought of doing such a thing? Who else would've even cared if a Viking boy lived or died?

"I've just realised something," I eventually say. "You're actually a good person, aren't you, Athelstan Cerdinga? Lots of people pretend they're good, like some of the fat priests preaching in the churches about sin while they make a comfortable living from the people they supposedly serve, but you're the real thing; you're actually good."

Athelstan looks embarrassed and shrugs again. "I don't know about that, and I won't hear anything bad said about the priests and the work they do for the good of our souls. Anyway, all I'm trying to do is help a boy who's in a bad situation that's no fault of his own. Anyone would do that."

"I'm not so sure," I say sceptically. "Most people would be glad to see a Viking die, boy or not."

"Well, obviously I'm not 'most people', I'm Athelstan and I won't let someone suffer if I can possibly help it."

That seems to be the last word on the subject and we set off for the frontier with Danelaw. It's a beautiful summer day with a bright and warm sun and for the next few hours we make good time on roads that are firm after a month or so without rain. The dark hours pass without incident and though we all laugh when Athelstan says we can set Bumble as guard dog to keep us safe, the little dog's ability to protect us isn't needed and we get a good night's sleep.

The next day we set out early, wanting to reach the border as soon as possible. Olaf is quiet, almost as though he's scared, but then I realise he's just nervous that something will go wrong and he won't get back to his people after all.

But he has nothing to worry about. That afternoon, Athelstan reins his tall horse to a halt and says, "We've just about arrived, I think."

"Arrived where?" I ask.

"The border with Danelaw."

"Oh," I say and look around at the low hills and peaceful green fields with stands of woodland. "But where's the... where's the wall or marker or whatever it is that says 'Mercia stops here' or 'You are now entering Danelaw: be prepared to get your head smashed in'?"

"Don't be daft," says Athelstan. "Who's going to put up a sign? The border's contested and can change at any time. It's made and held by armies and everyone knows where it is… more or less."

"Well I don't," I say argumentatively. "Just how can you tell we're at the border? Do the birds speak with a Danish accent? Does the wind smell of Viking farts?" I turn to Olaf. "Do you recognise the area?"

He shrugs. "How would I? I've never been here. My home's Denmark, not Danelaw."

"Look, just take my word for it. I've been told that a river divides Mercia from Danelaw and there it is," says Athelstan pointing at a muddy stream that's hardly deep enough to wet a pony's hooves.

I sigh. There's no point in arguing. Either we're about to cross into enemy territory or we're not. Anyway, I have a feeling we'll soon find out one way or another.

We continue for another two hours or so, and at last we reach the crest of a hill and look down on a large village that is nestled in the wide loop of a meandering river. Neatly laid out fields stretch away into the distance towards a stand of woodland, and the sounds of a barking dog, children laughing and a woman singing rise up to our position on the hill crest. An earth embankment topped with a wooden wall surrounds the village, showing it can be defended if needs be.

"So, Danish or Saxon?" says Athelstan.

"Danish," Olaf answers decisively.

"How can you tell?" I ask.

"Look at the centre. The cleared area for meetings. You can see the oak 'god pole' rising into the sky. It connects the Aesir or 'sky gods' with the Vanir or 'earth gods'. No Saxon settlement would have such a thing. You forgot your true gods long ago."

"Not all of us," I say quietly and for a moment I think I hear the call of ravens.

"Then that's settled it," says Athelstan. "Here we say goodbye, Olaf Swainson."

The words take a while to sink in, but then the three of us look at each other almost shyly. Boys of our age find partings like this difficult. Officially we're not allowed tears, in fact the best we can do is a punch on the shoulder, perhaps a handshake or if things get really emotional, maybe a manly hug. But we don't do any of that – we'd have to get off our horses and that's just going too far. But Bumble has no such barriers to his feelings. He knows something important is happening and that someone's leaving and he whines so much that we have to pass him around between the three of us while he snuggles up to our necks and licks our faces, making us so wet no one will know if there's anything other than doggy spit running down our cheeks.

Athelstan then reaches into his saddlebag and hands a purse over to Olaf. "You'll need this to pay for food and a passage back to Denmark. The coins will be accepted by your people. It's Danish gold taken from raiding dragon boats."

Olaf smiles his thanks. "Goodbye, Athelstan Cerdinga," he says, "When you're king, remember the Danes are people too."

"I will and do," Athelstan says quietly.

"And goodbye to you too, Edwin," he says. "I think you knew it already."

"I did and do too."

He nods, turns his pony towards the village and gallops away.

We watch for a while as Bumble whines quietly and then Athelstan says, "And we'd better hurry as well. The closer we are to the border before dark, the happier I'll be."

"Surely you don't think Olaf would…"

"No, of course not. But there are bound to be regular patrols in this frontier area and an atheling of the Royal House of Cerdinga would be a great prize for any Viking warrior."

I nod. He's right of course, but I'm not too worried. If there were any danger, I'm sure Ara of the Ravens would've made an appearance. Anyway, soon we're heading back over the fields and meadows towards the safety of Mercia.

XI

O n our way back to Tamworth we make a detour
to the village where we left the housecarles
and return together to find the city quiet. Without
the Lady Aethelflaed and the army, the place seems
somehow *deflated*. The streets are still busy and the
small shops and stalls are doing brisk business, but
there isn't the same sense of energy and purpose
that usually fills the settlement when the Lady of the
Mercians is at home and overseeing the running of
the kingdom.

We quickly settle back into our usual routine and
wait as impatiently as everyone else for news of the
attack on the Northumbrian Vikings. But all stays

quiet with no messengers and no reports of any sort for days.

But then at last on a bright sunny morning a rider clatters into the palace precinct and we all rush out to see who it is. With Lord Ethelred too ill to receive messengers, the rider asks for Athelstan and when he's pointed out the man hurries over to where we stand among a throng of chamberlains and officials of the royal household. He hands over a small roll of parchment and Athelstan breaks the seal and reads it quickly. He sighs with relief and smiles and then nods at the messenger who immediately turns to the small crowd that is continuing to gather in the palace precinct.

"VICTORY! WE HAVE A GREAT VICTORY OVER THE ENEMY! THE LADY AETHELFLAED AND KING EDWARD HAVE BROUGHT THE DANISH ARMY LOW AND DRIVEN THEM OVER THE LAND LIKE SHEEP!"

I listen as the cheer that begins at the palace flows down into Tamworth like a river in spate. Soon the sound washes back and breaks like a huge wave over us as we all laugh and hug each other. But over by the palace wall I see a dark figure with ravens. She stands quietly and I somehow know that the work has only just begun.

"So, Athelstan, I hear that you set free Olaf Swainson. Can this really be true?" The Lady Aethelflaed sits in her nephew's private chamber, her war-calloused hands folded in her lap and a small smile on her lips. It's more than three days since she returned victorious at the head of her army and she's waited until now to question us about the disappearance of the Viking hostage.

Athelstan sits opposite her, while I hover in the background with a ewer of wine, ready to fill their drinking horns. I feel as guilty as a kitten found with its head in the cream jug, but Athelstan holds his aunt's gaze and answers coolly, "I wasn't prepared to see him executed, Aunt. And letting him go before he could gather too much information about our future plans for war seemed the best thing to do."

"I see. Don't you think it would have been better if you'd consulted both myself and your father before you took this action?"

"No. As King of Wessex, my father hates all Danes. If I'd suggested setting Olaf free, he'd have killed him to prove how ruthless he can be and to 'toughen me up' as he's always saying."

"Don't you think I could have protected him from your father?"

"I don't know, perhaps. But I wasn't sure how you felt about Vikings yourself, and I wasn't prepared to risk my friend's life."

"Your friend? Is it possible for a Saxon and a Dane to be friends?" Aethelflaed says with an enquiring look on her face.

"More than *just* friends, I'd say, judging by the amount of half-Danish children we see even in the streets of Tamworth," Athelstan answers.

His aunt laughs. "Well, people will be people, given half a chance. So, yes, I suppose I know the answer to my own question, it is possible for Saxons and Danes to be friends. And, in fact, with that in mind, I've reached a conclusion about what to do when we've taken back the lands the Danes stole from us."

"Drive them out, I suppose," says Athelstan and I can hear a weary, almost sad note in his voice. "Cleanse the land of every last one of them and everything they've brought with them."

"You're not listening, oh nephew of mine," his aunt replies tartly. "To be a good ruler you need to hear and understand every word that's spoken, and all those that are not. I intend to invade Danelaw. And I mean to break all who come against us. But when they're defeated and accept us as their overlords and rulers, and when they've taken oaths of loyalty to the kings of Wessex and the rulers of Mercia, they can stay and make this land their home."

"Oh…" is all Athelstan can manage to say.

"Why are you surprised?" Aethelflaed asks. "If we drive out the Danes, the land will lie empty and even if we reseed it with Saxon people, the Vikings will return one day and fight wars to take it back, disrupting the land, killing the people and emptying the treasuries of gold. But if we let them stay and live, they become part of *our* land and *our* world. The Danish people are cousins to us anyway. We speak a language that's obviously from the same root. Before we became Christians we worshipped the same gods, and it's part of our history that we too came here in longboats and fought to make our homes on this land." She pauses and takes a drink of her wine, her eyes staring out across the room without focusing on anything. "You speak, Athelstan, of half-Danish children, a mixing of different blood, but I think it's clear that the blood of Saxon and Dane are almost identical. We're of the same family line."

"So after war with the Danes, there'll be peace," Athelstan says. "But what of the others on these islands, the Welsh, the Cornish, the Scots and those older people, the little dark folk who still live deep in the forests and high in the hills. Will you make peace with them too?"

"I've only one lifetime, oh nephew of mine! I have enough work to do taming the Danes. And who knows if a lasting peace can ever be made with the Scots and the Welsh and those others? Perhaps that's for you to find out, Athelstan Cerdinga, and for those who come after you. If it can be done, it'll take generations to do it, but I suppose we must start somewhere."

Not long after this, the Lady of the Mercians leaves and I sigh with relief. Bumble also emerges from his hiding place under the bed and wags his tail happily. But Athelstan sits in silence, his cheek resting on his fist and a frown on his face. I know his aunt's words echo similar ideas that he has, and he's deep in thought.

"Can I get you anything?" I ask.

"Yes, a time of quiet," he says but then smiles to show he didn't mean to snap. "No, just leave me with my thoughts."

I know he doesn't want to be alone in his room, so I play with Bumble as quietly as possible on the bed, while the strange boy I serve builds dreams of the future.

XII

A few days later something happens that means such dreams of the future will have to wait, as news reaches us of a huge Viking army descending on Mercia, intent on revenge for the defeat it's just suffered. Viking pride has been dented and the kings of Danelaw have gathered a huge fleet of ships that have cleverly sailed up the River Severn deep into the heartland of our territory. The first we know of it is when riders thunder into Tamworth, reporting that an enemy army has landed as far up the river as their dragon boats could go and that now they are laying waste to the land. Towns and villages are burning, farms are being destroyed and people are dying.

But the Vikings don't yet realise how much better prepared we are for their raids and attacks.

The people soon escape to the 'burghs' or defensive towns, where they're safe, and messengers have taken warnings not only to the capital of Mercia and the Lady Aethelflaed but also to Wessex and King Edward. His army is soon gathered and is marching north to our aid while our soldiers are preparing to march south.

But the army of Mercia will have with it Athelstan Cerdinga, Aethling of Wessex, a mighty warrior and possibly the next fighting king of that ancient domain. And with him too will be Edwin the shoemaker's son, who does his best when he has no choice but to fight.

I only find out we'll be included in the army as I'm making Athelstan's bed, ably helped by Bumble, who keeps burying his ball under the covers and then diving to the bottom of the bed as he tries to retrieve it. It's just as I'm trying to drag the small wriggling dog, plus ball, from out of the sheets that Athelstan bursts into the room.

"We're in, Edwin! We're in!"

"In what? The doghouse?"

"No! We're in the army that Aethelflaed's leading south! She's kept her promise about including us in the next campaign. Come on, pack your kit, grab your sword, shield and spear. We march in less than an hour!"

"It'll take me longer than an hour to pack your kit and mine," I say quietly. I'm never as enthusiastic about fighting as Athelstan is. The aristocrats and leaders of this world seem to see war as a sort of extreme sport. But I think fighting should be considered the worst failure any politician and leader can commit, because they've failed in their duty to protect the people and the land from war. I'll fight if I have to, and being body-servant to a Cerdinga, I suppose I'm going to have to do it a lot, but there are many other things I'd sooner do, like playing with Bumble for one or... well, actually I'd sooner do pretty much anything else, come to think of it.

"You can't take more than an hour. Just pack basics, there's no time for anything else!"

"Your sort of basics or mine?" I ask.

"Whichever's quickest!" he says and dives out the door.

"Mine then," I say to Bumble, who yaps in agreement.

I've heard the soldiers talk a lot about 'Roman Speed', but now I'm witnessing it. In fact I'm part of it as our army swings along through the Mercian countryside. I'm almost breathless with excitement and terrified at one and the same time. I'm riding my pony at the head of the army, just behind Athelstan, Lady Aethelflaed and some big bearded blokes who I presume are the generals. As it's summertime the roads are dry and therefore dusty, so my eyes are stinging and I can't stop coughing. I know I'm lucky though, because only the top officials are riding horses; everyone else walks, or rather marches.

Messengers have been galloping back and forth between us and the army of Wessex ever since we left Tamworth, and it's obvious the plan is for the two Saxon armies to meet and merge. Late in the afternoon more and more messengers arrive and I sense a growing excitement. The enemy has been spotted, and they're marching down a narrow valley towards a river crossing. If both our Saxon armies move fast we can trap them between us, closing on the Danes like the jaws of a hungry wolf.

Aethelflaed snaps out orders and the marching pace is increased so that we're swinging along like a man hurrying home for his dinner. But the commanders have to be careful here: if we move too quickly, the soldiers could be exhausted and unable to fight when we finally catch up with the enemy, but if we go too slowly the enemy could escape.

I look back over the column of the army that snakes along the road almost as far as I can see, and they all look determined and ready for a fight. But who knows how they'll feel after a couple of hours at this pace.

I needn't have worried. Ahead I can see a sort of cut across the land as though someone has taken a huge sword and gouged out a narrow slice through earth and rock. Judging by the intense discussions amongst the high command, this is obviously the valley that the messengers told us about. And just beyond this valley, I can see a cloud of dust rising up into the air that can only have been made by the army of Wessex hurrying along to meet us.

Aethelflaed sends out more messengers and also scouts to spy out a route that our soldiers can take to hit the enemy. And then suddenly everything seems to fall into place, the high command call a halt and dismount, and Athelstan waves me over to stand with him. I take up my position and I look around at the ranks that are forming into battle order. Then I see the spirit of Ara is with us, making her shape and form from the shadows around, while her ghostly ravens fly above us, their calls seeming to echo from a great distance.

The army now moves with the precision of oiled cogs to fan out over the land in a wide front that is four warriors deep. More orders are shouted and we move forward like one gigantic beast, scaled with overlapping shields and bristling with spears like spines.

We reach the lip of the valley and look down. I can clearly see the Viking army marching along the river that meanders across the valley floor, and less than half a mile away I can also see the army of Wessex, their banner of the white dragon flying in the wind. The Lady Aethelflaed raises her hand and our banner is unfurled so that the yellow wyvern of Mercia flies over our ranks.

Now our war horns begin to growl, and immediately the war horns of Wessex reply, filling the air with a deep booming that sends a shiver down my spine. Down in the valley the Danish army suddenly realises its danger and a great roar of defiance rises up from the men.

Aethelflaed lifts her sword and with a mighty war cry she leads us down into the valley at a swinging trot that eats up the ground. All the warriors of Mercia keep perfect pace with each other, presenting a solid wall of spears and shields. I can feel the rush of power that soldiers often talk about as the joy of battle fills me. I shout aloud, adding my voice to those of my comrades, our voices echoing over the air.

The Danes wait for us, their shield wall standing steady and their voices rising up in a fierce battle song that has a strong fighting rhythm. They beat their swords on their shields, the noise smashing against us as we advance over the land. Again Aethelflaed raises her sword and we give a huge shout and leap forward in the charge.

I can see the Vikings' fierce faces still singing their battle song, but then we hit them like a landslide of iron and the screeching roar of onset fills the air. The Danish wall is pushed back and we almost break through, but the enemy are brave and mighty fighters, and they drive their feet into the earth and push back against us, slowly straightening their line.

Athelstan's sword strikes again and again against the wall of shields and I match him stroke for stroke. A huge bearded face suddenly fills my world and an axe smashes down into my shield. I almost fall, but Athelstan grabs me, hauling me up, and I thrust my sword at the face making the Dane step back. I plant my feet firmly again and with a roar I hack at the man, catching his shield and driving him to his knees. His neck is exposed and I chop down hard. He falls at my feet and I step forward with the rest of the Saxon shield wall.

Then a huge clamour rises up and we know the army of Wessex has hit the Vikings on the opposite side of their stand. The Danes are now trapped between the anvil of Mercia and the hammer of Wessex and I watch as Aethelflaed calls her soldiers on, leading us forward in a charge that drives deep into the enemy line. All around us Danes are falling, but their kings rally them to their raven banner and they re-form the wall. Once again they begin to sing a fierce battle paean and we know they will not surrender. I look at Athelstan and he nods at me. "Nearly done, brother!"

"Nearly done," I agree.

But it's not. The Dane's re-formed shield wall stands solid and impregnable and no matter what we do to break through they repulse us again and again. The sun sinks slowly towards the horizon. If the enemy can hold out until darkness, they could slip away, taking their spoils of war with them and bragging of their prowess. But then the Lady of the Mercians calls us back to re-form our ranks. She barks an order and the war horns begin to growl again and then someone starts the war chant of the Saxons. The chant that's been heard in these islands for almost half a millennium:

"*OUT!* Out! Out! *OUT!* Out! Out! *OUT!* Out! Out!"

All our fighters take it up. Spitting out the word with power and venom. The simple barking sound smashing against the enemy shields like word-arrows. Then the Lady Aethelflaed turns to face us, her sword held aloft, her battered shield still unbroken and solid, and she throws back her head and lets out a high-pitched howl like a she-wolf calling her pack on to destroy and rend and kill.

We answer her call with a roar and we charge, hitting the enemy's wall with a fury. My head is filled with a raging, ravenous need to drive the Danes from our land. I offer no mercy, I feel no pity, my reluctance to fight is long-forgotten. I smash again and again at the shields before me, driving forward beside Athelstan who kills and kills everything before him.

Then at last we're through; the wall collapses, but again we see the bravery of the enemy as they fall back and once again re-form in a tight, crouching knot around their banner.

The Lady Aethelflaed calls out to them to lay down their arms but they roar defiance and fight on. My arm aches with the effort of raising my sword and hacking it down on the enemy. I'm drenched in Viking blood and still we push forward.

A giant of a man wearing the gold collar of a Danish king suddenly smashes into mine and Athelstan's shields, driving us back, but we immediately reply with a hail of sword strokes, one supporting the other as Athelstan strikes first and then I strike as he raises his sword ready for the next stroke. The Dane laughs aloud, but his eyes widen as I drive my sword deep into his guts. He falls backwards and as we advance he calls out:

"Finish it, boys. Valhalla awaits!"

"Then go, and tell them Athelstan Cerdinga sent you," my master says and thrusts deep.

Now three banners can be clearly seen as we close in on the enemy's last stand: the white dragon of Wessex with the yellow wyvern of Mercia against the black raven of the Danes.

The Vikings resist stubbornly, refusing the offer of surrender until Aethelflaed loses patience and driving forward she reaches the raven banner where the last of the Danish kings stands with his housecarles. This final stage of the battle is the fiercest and we stand toe to toe with our enemies, staring deep into the eyes of the warriors we kill. I'm almost exhausted, and I draw my breath with a whooping sound as I force myself to fight on.

But then I watch as Aethelflaed and King Edward of Wessex stride forward together and after a mighty struggle they hack down the last Danish king and his standard-bearer.

"It's done," Athelstan gasps.

I fall to my knees and nod while Ara's ravens call out our victory over the land.

XIII

So ended the Battle of Tettenhall. Countless thousands of Vikings fell that day. Three of their kings were killed and the few who escaped the battlefield were hunted down by the warriors of Wessex and Mercia. We showed no mercy. Some say the enemy will never send such a great army against us again. But I'm not so sure. The Danes are brave and stubborn fighters. If you chop the head off one of their dragons, it grows another one and you have to kill it all over again.

I made the journey back to Tamworth in silence. Athelstan tried to talk to me, but I could barely answer him. Eventually he put his cloak around my shoulders and then his arm as he realised just how horrible and hollow and even ashamed I felt. I'd fought and killed before, against the Viking fleet off the Wessex coast. But that had been nothing like the Battle of Tettenhall. I lost count of how many men I'd stabbed and hacked with my sword, and all of them would have been the sons of someone now grieving.

But as a soldier in the army of Mercia I quickly realised that I can't afford to feel like this. Or at least I can't afford to let it affect me so badly. I'm a friend and servant of the most important aethling in Wessex. One day he could be king and he'll probably spend most of his life fighting and marching off to wars. So I'll have to become the greatest warrior I can possibly be just to keep up with him.

Several months later, Ethelred the Ealdorman of Mercia and husband of Aethelflaed dies. The Witan officially appoint Aethelflaed as queen in everything but name, calling her the Lady of the Mercians. The people have called her this for years, and she's ruled the land on her own for just as long, so nothing is really different.

The years pass. Battles are fought and are either won or lost, alliances are made and unmade, treaties are sealed and broken. But while Athelstan and I grow stronger and broader, little Bumble grows fatter and becomes slower, so that soon he spends most of his time asleep, conserving his energy for a mad time of playing at bedtime.

Then one day, we get back to Athelstan's room to find Bumble is too tired to play. He wags his tail happily and yaps a greeting but he lays down his head and sighs. I suddenly realise he's almost reached the end of a life that's been full of fun and playing and love.

"Perhaps you should stroke him, Athelstan," I say.

"Why? I've been stroking him on and off all day."

"Yes, but... I think he's going to leave us soon," I answer.

My friend immediately gets up from the table where he's just settled down to read and hurries over to the bed where the little dog is lying. "What do you mean, 'leave us'? He can't die yet. I've had him for ever. When he goes he'll take my boyhood with him."

He strokes Bumble's head and the little creature licks his hand. We stay with him while the candles slowly burn down, then just as the sun begins to set, he suddenly opens his eyes, gives a little yap as though to say goodbye, and when his tail stops wagging we know he's died.

Neither of us sleeps that night as we mourn for the little scrap of a dog that's been part of our lives for so long. People say it's daft to grieve over an animal, but I say love deserves to be acknowledged no matter where it's found; there's too little in the world and what there is should be given proper respect.

Now begins a time of great battles against the Vikings. King Edward takes East Anglia from the Danes and Aethelflaed attacks Danelaw, capturing Derby and accepting the surrender of Leicester. The fighting is fierce, and Athelstan and I take part in many of the Lady of the Mercians' campaigns. My master is now a trusted part of his aunt's war councils and he is helping to plan and build burghs throughout Mercia.

And what about me? Well, I'm still Edwin the shoemaker's son. Though now I'm respected in the Mercian court, and because I don't use my friendship with Athelstan to make myself richer or more powerful, I'm quite well liked. I'm still body-servant to my master and haven't wanted anything more. I have all the wealth I need and I'm not interested in power. I have the honour of standing next to him in the shield wall and I fight beside him whether we're on land or sea. Though when we're on board ship I spend a lot of my time hanging over the side, losing my breakfast or whatever other meal I've just had.

At present we're living at the palace in Tamworth where Aethelflaed is resting after being wounded during her latest campaign. The best healers in the country are attending her, and some have even crossed the seas from Europe. Nobody seems too worried; it's to be expected that a great warrior like the Lady of the Mercians will be injured at some point. In fact she's been wounded many times and has always recovered, so why should it be different this time? At least that's what I say to Athelstan, though I hear ravens calling everywhere, and Ara stands in the shadows of the Lady's chamber.

I've just finished getting my master's room ready for the night and I'm thinking about going to get some supper when Athelstan comes back from the meeting he's been having with the army's high command.

"Whatever it is you're doing, leave it. Aethelflaed wants us."

I'd be surprised if she wanted me, but I know that what Athelstan really means is that *he* wants me. His aunt must've taken a turn for the worse. Like all royalty, Athelstan has spent hardly any time with his parents over the years of training and fighting, so Aethelflaed, his aunt and teacher, is the closest thing he has to a mother. If she dies he'll be crushed.

As we approach the Lady's chamber we have to force our way through a crowd of chamberlains and other officials. Everyone knows that a change is about to happen, and for a palace servant that can either mean an opportunity for advancement or the loss of any status they already have. The lives of those of us who serve the great and powerful can be precarious; if our masters and mistresses fall, so do we, and when they die, we must find others to serve or risk spending our lives in poverty. Even though I know this to be true, I can't help being reminded of carrion beasts gathering around a corpse, as these servants and retainers begin their manoeuvrings for new positions and security.

But as we get nearer to the Lady's room, I see there are others present, and I clearly hear the lilt of a Danish accent.

"Viking envoys from York," Athelstan explains. Aunt was... *is* planning to attack Northumbria again and take back the city into Saxon control. They know they have no chance against her, so they're here to surrender and accept her as their overlord... or perhaps I should say over*lady*."

I nod but say nothing. I wonder if they'll still be here if the worst happens and Aethelflaed dies.

Inside the chamber the air is thick with the sweet smell of incense, but even so it can't hide the fact that there's another smell, equally sweet and horribly sickening. Aethelflaed's wounds have become infected and the healers have lost their battle.

What can I say? There's no death-bed speech, no tearful farewells. We arrive just in time to see the Lady of the Mercians take one last juddering breath and then lie still. I watch as the news of her death flies off and through the palace. The waiting women began to wail, the priests start to chant and soon I hear the first church bells tolling beyond the precinct. But it's the sight of Ara of the Ravens stepping forward from the shadows and leading off something or *someone* I can't quite see that finally convinces me that the mighty fighting soul of Aethelflaed Cerdinga has finally left her body.

I look at Athelstan, ready to give comfort, but before I can say anything a chamberlain forces his way into the already crowded room and whispers in my master's ear. He turns to me.

"The Viking envoys from York have gone, taking their surrender with them. If that particular jewel is ever to be remounted into a Saxon setting, we'll have to fight to get it."

I nod completely unsurprised. I'd suspected this might happen.

The mourning time for Aethelflaed is short; the Vikings wait for no one's funeral and any sign of weakness will have them crossing the borders in their droves. Even so, there is a little time to say goodbye to the Lady of the Mercians, and I'm with Athelstan when he stands beside her coffin and promises that he will win back York for her and the Saxons.

But the fight for that Viking city has to wait. Athelstan doesn't yet have the authority to lead an attack and without Aethelflaed something of the drive and determination for the campaign is lost. But the time will come, and we must be ready when it does.

XIV

Over the next few years our lives change beyond recognition. With the deaths of Ethelred and Aethelflaed of Mercia, power passes from the older generation. Then King Edward Cerdinga of Wessex, my master's father, also dies and the Witan elect Athelstan as the new king. For me this shift of power began humbly when Bumble passed, something that seemed to bring our boyhood to an end, and now this latest death places the responsibilities and burdens of manhood firmly on Athelstan's shoulders. I am now body-servant and also friend to one of the most powerful rulers in these islands!

I'm overseeing the royal household's journey from the capital of Winchester to the ancient town of Kingston-upon-Thames where all the kings of Wessex are anointed as king. I'm so excited as the coronation approaches that I almost forget to send off the newly made robes and regalia for the special day. I know this sounds unlikely, but after a while one crate looks much like another, even if one contains only bedding and another the coronation robes of the new king of the land.

You can be sure I say nothing about this to anybody and especially not to Athelstan. As far as the rest of the household is concerned, the whole operation goes as smoothly as oiled silk.

The night before the ceremony a great feast is held in the incredibly old and shabby Mead Hall of Kingston. But every one of the royal chamberlains does their best to make the place look splendid and soon the cracked plaster and flagstones of the hall are covered by beautiful tapestries, and where the new king will sit at the head of the top table, a real carpet imported from the fabled land of Persia itself is laid where the royal feet will rest.

That night in Athelstan's chamber there's an air of just-suppressed excitement. But none of it seems to come from the man himself. He's as sober as he should be the night before he's crowned, but he shows no sign of nerves.

"Sit, Edwin, and for goodness' sake, take some wine and calm down!" he orders, and I draw up a stool to the room's small table opposite my friend and newly elected king.

"Will you have some?" I ask, raising the jug.

"No. I need to have a clear head for tomorrow," he answers and I nod.

"I hear the Archbishop of Canterbury had trouble on the road," I eventually say.

"What happened, did his horse collapse under him?" says Athelstan with a snort of laughter. "I've never seen a man as fat as him: so much for priests being 'moderate in their diet' as the rulebooks of the church say."

"Perhaps he ate the books before he read them," I suggest.

"Perhaps. But I suppose we should talk of him with more respect. He *is* the most senior churchman in all the land as well as being in charge of the coronation ceremony tomorrow."

"All right," I agree. After all there aren't many in these cold, wet islands who can say they've been to the mighty city of Rome and been ordained a priest by the Pope himself.

"Anyway, you said he had a problem. What happened?"

"His horse *did* collapse under him and die."

"You're joking!"

I shake my head.

"Did he eat it?" Athelstan asks.

The coronation is as splendid as I hoped it would be. Athelstan refuses a horse and walks through the streets of the town leading the thegns, ealdormen and other dignitaries to the church of All Saints. As his body-servant I hold the hem of the long, gold-embroidered cloak of his coronation robes and can't help grinning like an idiot as the huge crowds cheer our procession.

We're preceded by chanting priests who swing incense holders that fill the air with scented smoke and purify the man who will soon be consecrated as king. Ahead I can see the raised wooden platform outside the church where Anhelm, the Archbishop of Canterbury, will perform the rites.

Athelstan has spent some time discussing the ritual with the archbishop and I suspect he's added some touches of his own that he's keeping secret.

We reach the platform and Athelstan steps up into full view and waves to the crowds before sitting on the waiting throne, the seat of which is made of stone; *the* kingstone, in fact, that the town takes its name from and on which generations of Saxon kings have sat during their coronations.

The ceremony drones on with a fog of incense and chanting, but then at the height of the ritual, the archbishop takes a circlet of gold and places this 'crown' upon the new king's head. This is the first time such a thing has been done in a coronation. Before this the highlight of the ceremony came when the priest poured holy oil on the new king's head, making him 'God's anointed'.

Now the reality of running a kingdom that's almost constantly at war overtakes us and Athelstan settles to his rule as he begins the task of showing that he's worthy of his new role. His long training with the Lady Aethelflaed stands him in good stead and he proves himself a clever king. He signs a treaty with Sitric, the Viking king of York, but when the elderly king dies, his son refuses to honour the agreement his father signed and I have to wonder if Athelstan knew this would happen. But whether he did or not, Wessex finally has the perfect reason to invade Northumbria and attack York.

The new phase of the continuing wars between Saxons and Danes begins and we travel over the land like a storm-driven winter wind, the army eating up the miles as though the devils of hell are after us. I'm sure the Vikings know we're coming, but when we arrive outside the Roman walls of York, they seem surprised. There are workmen still rebuilding the battlemented tops of one section of the defences and as we draw nearer we can see the gates are still open and carts are trundling through.

Athelstan calls his generals together, and as the king's companion I stand with them while they discuss how they'll take the city. As ever in these times of crisis and conflict, Ara is there too, a raven sitting on each shoulder so that she looks like some three-headed beast of nightmares.

"Well, Algar Godwinson, this looks like a strong wall to break," Athelstan says to the most experienced of the high command. "It's sixty years since the Danes captured the city from the Saxons and it looks like they've spent a good part of that time making the defences higher and stronger. They'll be hard to crack."

"No worse than some, and probably easier than others, I reckon," the old soldier answers. "Though there's some in the army who're too young to know that. They'll be nervous looking at all these stone walls and iron-reinforced gates."

"Then the sooner we hit them, the less time the men will have to worry about it," Athelstan replies.

The sun is just rising, sparking rainbows from the dew-drenched grass and sending a scent of damp earth and wild flowers into the cool air. Then, despite the urgent need to move quickly, the king pauses for a moment and looks back over his army that stands on the flat land surrounding the city. They're well armed and well trained and at their head is a party of sturdy housecarles who carry between them a massive battering ram made from the trunk of a mighty oak tree. It's slung on a network of cradling ropes that'll be used to swing its huge weight against the city's defences.

The king nods as though satisfied at last, and then striding forward he raises his sword and gives the word to advance.

Immediately a great roar rises up from the army of Wessex and Mercia and the war-horns of the Danish defenders on the walls begin to boom their warnings. Athelstan leads the army around the walls to the eastern gate of the city, while the defenders rain down arrows and spears on us as we swing by. But we're out of range and none of us falls.

Within a short while the east gate of the city rises up before us like a cliff face made of bricks and dressed stone. The legions of the old Roman Empire had built the massive entranceway into the city, and though it's old, I can see it's as strong as the day it was built. But the wooden leaves of the gates themselves are new, the thick planks that make up their width gleaming almost white in the early morning sunlight. They're studded with the black iron of nail heads and bolts, and spreading three-quarters of the way across their width are six mighty hinges, three to each leaf. I almost feel like running away at the sight of the gates we must break. But I swallow hard and stand firm.

Athelstan calls a halt, gathers his war band of elite companions around him, including me, and nods at the defences.

"In any wall, the gate is always the weakest point, so this is where we must break into the city," the king says lightly, as though discussing the weather.

"It doesn't look overly weak to me," I say eyeing the battlements and fighting platform that runs along the top of the gate's high archway. The entire structure is crammed with Danish defenders.

"No," the king agrees. "But even so, it's here we must break in. The walls will be even tougher to breach. Who'll come with me to protect the battering ram?"

"I suppose that'll be all of us," I say reluctantly, looking over the rest of the companions for agreement and knowing that none of the elite band will risk the dishonour of refusing to go with the king. They've only just been appointed and still have to prove their prowess. In a way we're trapped by our sense of duty.

Athelstan nods, and turning he waves up the party of thirty housecarles who carry the battering ram between them. Now he raises his sword and gives the order to charge. Immediately the entire army leaps forward in support of the ramming party and at their head runs the king and his war band. Soon we're in range of the defenders and the air around us is thick with flying spears, arrows, axes and rocks, but on we run, the huge mouth of the gateway looming larger and wider the closer we get.

The roar of our war cry fills the entire world around us and back crashes the Viking reply. The gates are close now and the king runs at a low crouch like a racing greyhound, and with him run the real hounds of the war-dog pack, snarling and howling. We draw closer and closer to the gates; the ramming party seems unaware of the weight of the huge tree they carry, but the defending Danes target them, bringing many of them down, slowing the momentum of the charge. But the warriors of the surrounding army quickly step in to take their place and the ram surges on. As usual my earlier fears and doubts have fallen away as the frenzy of battle fills me to the brim. Soon the gates are near enough for us to smell the resinous scent of the newly cut wood. But the defenders throw spears and axes in a dense hail that brings down more and more of our men, so that a trail of corpses clearly shows the route of the ram's charge.

But then at last with a cry of triumph we smash into the wood of the mighty gates. A massive 'BOOM!' rises up into the air and the gates shudder like the shivering pelt of a living beast, but they hold. The ramming party falls in a heap and all around us spears and rocks rain down from the towering arch of the gatehouse. Athelstan raises his shield and we all do the same, making a sheltering roof while the rammers climb to their feet, draw back and smash forward again. BOOM! Again the gates hold and now the Danish defenders waiting on the road just inside the walls run forward to brace the huge leaves of wood, throwing themselves bodily against them as the ram draws back yet again. BOOM! And still the gates hold.

Athelstan now leads his war band to hack at the wood with massive axes, weakening it further.

"SMASH IT DOWN! SMASH IT DOWN!" he roars at the top of his lungs. And the housecarles wielding the ram respond, drawing back and swinging forward like a powerful and unstoppable storm-wave. BOOM! But still the gates stand and our warriors are falling under the rain of arrows and axes.

Suddenly Athelstan leaps up on to the huge ram and I scramble after him, determined to protect him if I can. He points his axe at the unmoving gates as he roars out a battle cry. The men of his war band now grab the ropes that girdle the tree trunk, and together with the housecarles they draw back the massive ram. Then with a roar the entire army surges forward, adding weight and power to the ram. BOOM! A rending screech rises up into the air as the wood of the gates begins to buckle.

The ram is swung back again and the army moves with it as one, and again the men rage forward and hit the gates like the hammer of the god Thunor. BOOM! And now CRACK! And now SCREECH! And now a high-pitched scream, like some living creature's death rattle, as the very fabric of the wood is torn apart and at last the gates burst open.

Athelstan leaps down from the ram with a triumphant roar and I follow as he leads his army into the streets of York, where the Danes are waiting for us in disciplined ranks. The king heads a charge that smashes into the enemy's wall of shields, driving them back for a moment before orders are rapped out and their lines slowly straighten.

Spears and throwing axes fly through the air, burying themselves deep into the flesh of Saxon and Dane alike. The dead and wounded fall, before they're dragged aside to allow the next warrior to take their place in the wall of shields.

So begins a long day's fighting with the Danes doggedly defending every street, and retreating only when a position can no longer be defended.

On and on for hours we keep open our lines of communication and secure each and every new gain before advancing again. But then our advance stalls and the cobbles beneath our feet run slick with blood as the Vikings counter-attack and try to drive us back in turn. Suddenly Athelstan slips and falls full-length in the blood and filth. Immediately the Danes surge forward to rend him where he lies. Without thinking I run and stand astride him, my sword singing as it hacks aside spear, axe and blade, then falls silent as the ringing is quenched in Danish flesh.

Athelstan climbs to his feet and now stands with me, driving back the enemy, until our line re-forms and we push forward again. For a moment he turns to me and smiles, as he raises the hilt of his sword to his brow in salute, and instantly it seems we're boys again, fighting our first battle against the Danish dragon boats, when Athelstan saluted me in exactly the same way after I saved him from a Viking axe.

The day wears on, until at last, as the red ball of the evening sun hangs over the streets and sends long shadows deep into the distance, the last of the Danes are surrounded in a great central square that had originally been laid out by the Romans.

Athelstan now gives an order and horns ring out over the city. We step back from our foe and a silence descends that's broken only by the laboured breathing of the exhausted fighters and the groans of the wounded and dying.

The king steps forward and raises his voice to battle pitch. "Soldiers of York, this battle is over: lay down your arms and kneel to me in fealty!"

A silence falls that's so deep, birdsong can be heard beyond the walls of the city. But slowly a murmuring rises up and a huge, grey-bearded Viking steps out from the enemy ranks and laughs. "Why should we give fealty to a Saxon?!"

"Because I am your king, by right of conquest and because the fighting is over and the wounded must be tended, the dead must be buried and the city repaired so that life may begin here again."

"And why should we die like cattle, executed by the spears of the Saxons, when we can die fighting and take our place in Valhalla and the halls of the gods?" the grey-beard asks again.

Athelstan holds the Viking's fierce gaze and replies quietly, "This battle is over and no more shall die. Lay down your arms and save those of the wounded who can be saved and begin the rebuilding that must be done."

The grey-beard laughs again. "We'll die here where we stand rather than work as slaves to the Saxons in a city that once was ours!"

"Swear fealty to me and you will work as free citizens of York, the city that will remain yours," Athelstan replies, his voice echoing over the square.

Once again a great murmuring rises up from the Danes and some call out to accept the terms offered by their enemy. But the grey-beard's still suspicious. "How can we know you won't kill us when we're disarmed? How can we know you're to be trusted?"

Athelstan looks over the defeated Vikings and says proudly, "Because I give you my word: the word of a king; the word of a king of the Royal House of Cerdinga; the word of *your* king!"

Silence falls once more and Athelstan holds the gaze of the grey-beard again until at last the quiet is broken by a single voice calling out:

"Listen to him. I know this king; he's a man of honour who will keep his word."

I look for the speaker and watch as a tall man steps out of the Viking ranks. He looks familiar somehow and I stare at him as I try to remember where I've seen him before.

"I was held hostage by the Saxons of Mercia, but when King Athelstan feared they might kill me, he set me free, even riding into Danelaw itself to do it."

"Olaf!" I shout, recognising him at last. And forgetting myself I hurry forward. "Olaf Swainson!" I say as I stand before him, and without thinking we both hug each other as though we're long-lost brothers.

The silence is intense as I lead him to where Athelstan stands. "Hello, Olaf," he says simply and smiles as though we've all just met in a tavern.

"Hello, Athelstan Cerdinga, my lord and king," the Viking answers, and falling to one knee he places his sword in Athelstan's hands.

A cheer then rises up from our ranks, and as one the Danish citizens of York fall to their knees and bow their heads to Athelstan. But above even the cheering, I can hear Ara's ravens exulting in the sky and also her cackling voice echoing over our victory.

This is the last Viking stronghold to fall to the Saxons, finally making Athelstan the first king of a united land known as England.

XV

Athelstan is now acknowledged as king from the south coast of Wessex to the border with Scotland and the kingdom of Strathclyde. And even beyond that, King Constantine of the Scots and Owain of the Strathclyde Welsh accept him as their overlord. His rule also stretches from the coasts of East Anglia and Northumbria in the east to the borders of Wales in the west, where their kings offer fealty and pay tribute to him.

His power is such that he issues coins that declare him King of the English and some even proclaim him as the first ruler of all Britain. After campaigning in Scotland and imposing his will on all who live in these islands, he sees peace at last settle over the land.

I watch now as this mighty king lies on his bed, his hands behind his head and his legs crossed while his expensive shoes drop mud all over the embroidered coverlet. It'll be my job to try and clean that up later.

We've just got back from a law-making ceremony where the kings of Scotland, Strathclyde and Wales were summoned to witness Athelstan's signature. The atmosphere was tense as Athelstan proved his power to all when his subject-rulers were forced to stand forward and swear an oath that they had duly witnessed his signature. After that, Athelstan smiled brightly and dismissed everyone from his presence, king and commoner alike.

I remember hearing the thunder of hooves as the Welsh and Scottish kings rode away back to their borders, and I felt a shudder travel the length of my spine. There may be no fighting at the present time on these islands, but I couldn't help thinking that we only held peace as a hostage rather than as an honoured and much-loved guest. The hatred I felt coming from the Scots and the Strathclyde Welsh during the law-making ceremony would find a way to express itself, and I didn't think it would be by means of harsh words and annoyance!

"Not a good feeling at the law-making today, Edwin," the king suddenly says.

"So you felt it too, then?"

"How could you miss it?" he says, sitting up and wiping more mud off his boots on to the coverlet as he does so. "The problem is if I don't act like the paramount ruler of these islands, the other kings will think me weak and rebel, and war will begin again. But if I *do* behave like a king above all other kings, it's understandably resented and so war becomes ever more likely."

"So, what can you do?" I ask.

"Wait for the inevitable war."

"Is that it? Can't you do anything else?"

"No. It's obvious the Scots and the Strathclyde Welsh are egging each other on to take action. It's just a matter of time before it begins. There needs to be another decisive battle in which the situation as it stands now is either confirmed, and I remain King of the English and paramount ruler, or it's all smashed apart, I'm killed and the Saxon people stand in danger of being enslaved by their Celtic neighbours. And no doubt, the Vikings will help to bring it all about."

"Oh… as simple as that, eh?"

"Yes, as simple as that," he answers easily.

I tidy the room in silence for a while and then remember I have something to give to Athelstan. I excuse myself, go to the storeroom where I've left it and then come back with the basket under my arm.

"For you," I say without ceremony and then watch as Athelstan's face lights up. He's still just like the boy I first met when it comes to presents.

"For me?" he says eagerly and takes the basket on to his lap. When a fat little body and squashed face emerges as he opens the lid, the king gasps aloud. The little dog then yaps in reply, wags his tail and licks Athelstan Cerdinga, the first ruler of all Britain, until he has to hold the squirming scrap of doghood high above his head in defence.

"I thought we could call him Rumbletump," I say. "What do you think?"

"Perfect," Athelstan replies, a wide smile illuminating his face. "We can shorten it to Rumble." Then he falls back on to the bed and allows the daft little creature to jump all over him.

I smile to myself, happy in the knowledge that this is just what he needs to take his mind off the world and all of its troubles.

The trouble, when it does come, still takes us by surprise even though we've been waiting for it to happen.

We're in one of the more comfortable royal palaces in Winchester, the capital of Wessex, and Athelstan is fighting in the lists, honing the battle skills he knows he's soon going to need, and I'm with him. Interestingly, the king is also overseeing a new sort of fighter he's training, after reading one of many books he owns that tell of the lives of the people of ancient Greece and Rome. He has more than six books that he's personally commissioned from the monks who copy and rebind them in the 'scriptorium' of the holy city of Canterbury. One of these told him of a Greek general in the city of Corinth who defeated the mighty Spartan army by using soldiers who would run at their enemy and throw light spears called javelins. They'd then run to safety before the enemy could catch them.

With this information in mind, Athelstan personally chose young men and women who are fast runners, and for the past few months he's been training them so that they can throw specially made light spears over huge distances and with great accuracy. Who knows if they'll be effective or not, but somehow I think we'll soon find out.

We're watching these javelin throwers running at targets when we realise that there's another running figure that's coming towards us. At first I think one of the soldiers is trying to assassinate Athelstan and I quickly draw my sword, but the king rests his hand on my arm.

"It's a messenger, you donkey," he says with a smile.

But I don't smile in return; I feel my stomach roll over and I draw a shuddering breath. This could be the news we've been waiting for and fearing for so long.

The man skids to a halt before us, gasping for breath. "My Lord, we're invaded! A great army has landed on the peninsula of the Wirral, between North Wales and the south of Cumbria."

"Who and how many?" Athelstan asks calmly.

"The Scots, the Vikings of Dublin and the Welsh of Strathclyde."

"And the Welsh of Cymru?" he asks, using the Welsh name for Wales.

"No, My Lord. Their kings have not crossed their borders."

He looks at me with a quick smile. "That's something at least. The kings of Wales aren't joining with their Welsh-speaking cousins of Strathclyde in this war. No doubt they're waiting to see who gets the upper hand before they make their move."

"The messenger hasn't told us how many there are yet," I point out, trying to keep the tremor of fear out of my voice.

Athelstan turns back to the man. "Well?"

"My Lord, their numbers couldn't be counted there are so many. I'm told that it is the greatest army to march over this land since the time of the Romans."

"I'll need more detail than that," the king says sharply, showing for the first time how stressed he must be. "I'll expect the next messengers to bring accurate figures and details of the enemy's defences and positions."

He then turns and walks back to the palace where he immediately calls a council of war. But if anyone expects King Athelstan Cerdinga to hurry off to battle before he's good and ready, they're soon disappointed. For the next week, he sends out the call to all points of Wessex and Mercia and then settles to train the soldiers already present in Winchester while he calmly waits for the rest of his army to muster. Many of his generals urge him to strike immediately, before the great army of Celts and Vikings can dig itself into defensive positions, but Athelstan refuses. He knows his own mind and exactly what he intends to do.

Then at last, just when I'm sure the high command and generals are about to rebel, the army is fully gathered and the march to the north begins.

XVI

Once we're on the road, the army moves at Roman Speed again and the miles roll by at a surprising rate. We arrive in Chester, the last big settlement before we reach the enemy, and find the city in a state of panic. But the presence of the king with his army calms down some of the people at least. Though this doesn't last long when they realise that the invaders heavily outnumber us, and that if we're defeated, Chester will be the enemy's first target.

It's almost a relief to march out the next morning and begin the last push that will bring us to battle. It's as we cross the peninsula called the Wirral that we first see signs of the enemy's presence, with burned-out farms and villages and the roadside littered with corpses.

At night we camp on the edge of the salt flats that eventually lead to the sea where the invading army waits. We set a strong guard and try to sleep, but I lie awake all night, listening to the wind howling like souls of the dead. How many more will add their voices to the dismal chorus by this time tomorrow?

We're up and ready before dawn. The wind's blowing from the sea that's less than a mile away and it's freezing and smells of salt. Overhead I can hear the croaking of crows and ravens mingling with the screams of gulls.

I've dressed Athelstan in his best war gear, and placed the circlet of gold around the crown of his helmet. He looks like a warrior-king should; he looks like the grandson of King Alfred, the first Saxon to defeat the Danes and he looks like the nephew of Aethelflaed, the Lady of the Mercians, who trained him and helped to lead the fightback against the Norsemen who'd taken almost half the land of these islands.

He stands now in the entrance of the campaign tent we've shared for the last few nights and smiles grimly. "Well, Edwin, are you ready to be bait in the trap?"

"No," I answer sullenly. "But as there's no choice, I suppose we'd better go and spring that trap."

"I suppose we better had. Stay close by me."

I follow him and see Ara of the Ravens, dark against a sky that's just beginning to pale towards dawn. Her face is set in grim lines of determination. I nod in greeting, but she turns and stares over the shadowed land to where the enemy waits.

The Mercian soldiers of our allied army have already marched out. I don't know why; all I can say is that they're part of Athelstan's plan, the trap for which we, the soldiers of Wessex, are the bait. We march towards the sea carrying torches. There's no need for secrecy; everyone knows the battle will be fought today. I look back over our ranks from where I march beside the king and I can see torches tailing off into the dark like the scales of a fiery dragon. Even so, without the Mercian contingent, our force looks pathetically small.

I search the darkness to see if I can see the Mercians, but there's nothing. Perhaps their part in the plan needs secrecy after all.

As ordered, I'm staying close to Athelstan, in fact I'm marching next to him and we're both surrounded by his war band: tall broad men with faces like a bad day in hell.

The eastern sky behind us is slowly growing lighter as dawn approaches, while ahead I can begin to see the faintest glimmerings of what I guess are the watch-fires of the enemy. They're tiny and scattered at first, but as we draw slowly nearer they begin to fill the darkness more and more, like a galaxy of stars spreading far and wide over the land. My heart starts to beat faster and louder as I begin to understand exactly what we're facing; three nations stand against us and the line of their armies presents a front that seems as wide as the world itself! How can we hope to win? I turn my head to the left and right as I run my eyes over the huge flowing sweep of watch-fires and I almost whimper aloud. But then I feel a hand rest on my shoulder.

"Steady, Edwin the shoemaker's son," Athelstan says quietly. "We're the bait, don't forget. We've got to look beatable and at the same time *believable* as an army that thinks it can win the battle. We've got to tempt them into committing all their forces into the fight, because that's when the Mercians will take them by surprise and hit them in the left and right flanks."

"Is that where they've gone, then?" I ask. "I know the Mercians marched off into the night, but I couldn't guess where they were going or why."

"They've split into two contingents," the king explains. "One section's marching to the north and one to the south. But they've had to take a wide sweep to keep out of the enemy's sight, so it'll take them a good while before they're in position and ready to strike."

"How long?"

"Hours."

"So we'll have to hold the enemy for all that time and make them fully engage with us. But how can we be certain they won't hold back any reserves that they'll bring out against the Mercians when they attack?"

"Because we're going to make so much noise and swagger they'll think we're the entire force. And not only that, we're going to offer them a prize they won't be able to resist: a prize they'll want so badly they'll forget about being cautious, and commit all of their reserves and their power to the battle to get it," the king answers.

"And what will that be... What *could* that be?"

"Me."

I glance at my master and see him smiling in the slowly growing dawn light. "I'm the tempting titbit on the delicious dish of revenge that's about to be set out before them. I'm Athelstan Cerdinga, the first King of the English, the hated one who's even called himself the first ruler of all Britain. The man who's made them accept him as their overlord, who's made them pay tribute to him and who's called them to attend his court like little lapdogs. How can they resist the temptation to smash me on the field of battle, especially when I'm arrogant enough to think I can face them with a ludicrously small force of soldiers? They think I'm already beaten; they can almost believe I'm already hacked to pieces under their swords and axes. It's just a matter of time before they're rid of me and all the Saxon scum who infest these islands."

"And could they be right... about you being already dead and the Saxons driven out I mean?" I ask quietly.

"The answer to that is only known to God, for the present. But we'll know too, soon enough."

I look ahead to the vast sweep of enemy watch-fires and try to believe that the answer will be the one we want. "I suppose we'd better go and play our part then."

Athelstan nods. "At least getting them to believe we're stupid enough to attack with such small numbers shouldn't be too difficult. They all think we're arrogant anyway; swaggering boldly into battle is exactly what they'll *expect* us to do."

And with that the king raises his hand and immediately dozens of war horns throughout our lines begin to boom over the early morning air. At the same time a huge bright red banner is unfurled showing the white dragon of Wessex that rages against the slowly lightning sky. "The sooner we let them know we're coming, the better," Athelstan says with a grim smile.

We march on over land that slowly becomes drier and firmer as tough sea grasses begin to take over from the reed beds and marshes. The wind is still blowing from the sea, bringing with it a scent of salt, and also the strangely musty smell of the thousands of warriors who wait for us. Overhead the ravens and crows keep pace with our march, their voices competing with the war horns that still echo over the air.

It's now so light that the great sweep of the enemy's watch-fires grows pale and soon dwindles to nothing, the light snuffed out like candles by the rising sun. But now at last, as I look ahead I get my first proper glimpse of the army that has sworn to drive us from the land, and it's all I can do not to weep. The army seems to fill the entire horizon from north to south. The watch-fires may have filled the darkness and made me wonder at the size of the force we were facing, but the actual sight of so many warriors standing in so many ranks in the full light of day is overwhelming. I gasp aloud and then begin to cough uncontrollably as I choke on my own spit.

"Steady up, Edwin," the king says, gripping my shoulder for a second time as I almost panic at the enemy's numbers. "They're just human like everyone else... They'll bleed, they'll die."

"Yes, but so will we," I manage to croak eventually.

Athelstan looks at me. "I think not... not today."

"How can you know?"

"Because we're meant to be here. This is a land of many peoples and some of those people are Saxon." He then raises his hand again and his war band begins to chant the old simple war cry that our people have sung over countless battlefields for hundreds of years:

"*OUT*! Out! Out! *OUT*! Out! Out! *OUT*! Out! Out!"

Soon the chant is taken up by the housecarles and then by the soldiers of the fyrd and the short sharp word is spat out again and again, a weapon that cracks over the air like a whip:

"*OUT!* OUT! OUT! *OUT!* OUT! OUT! *OUT!* OUT! OUT!"

The reply of the enemy begins to rise and swell from their ranks. They look like a huge storm cloud on the horizon, each individual made tiny by distance, but the wind is blowing towards us from the sea, so that we can clearly hear the enemy's war horns and the high, howling battle cries of the Scots that slice like glittering blades through the air. But over that, the singing of the Strathclyde Welsh drifts over the air. Even as I march towards their spears and swords and my probable death

I can't help but be moved by the beautiful singing of the Strathclyde Welsh.

"Ah, listen to that. Their voices are as sweet as the singing of the sirens," Athelstan says. I have no idea what he's talking about so I say nothing.

"Still, they must be silenced," he goes on. "But when we're all friends again, perhaps I'll hire Welsh singers for the royal Mead Halls!"

I stare at him. When we're all friends again! When have we ever been friends? Not only that, but does he really think that we'll even survive the battle, let alone win it and then be strong enough to order Welsh singers to perform in the royal palaces?! Sometimes I think that to be a king you need to be more than a little mad.

We march on. We're close enough now for me to see that the enemy stands in three definite sections. Banners fly above them like wild, raving birds in the wind from the sea. The Scots stand in the centre, their war banner rising above them, and the warriors beneath it shake their spears, axes and swords at us and the high yelps of their war cries rise into the air and mingle with the calls of the gulls that wheel around the skies above them.

On the right wing stand the Danes under their raven banners. Their shield wall stretches in an unbroken line and bristles with spears, each blade honed to razor-sharpness. They're mainly silent, but every few seconds a strange bellow erupts from their ranks and seems to punch the very air so that a surge of sound travels over the land and breaks against us like a wave at sea against a rock.

The Welsh hold the left wing, their voices swelling and rolling around the air as though the sky itself has found a voice and sings fiercely of war and death.

We continue to march, our shields locked together, and we flow over the shape of the land like the tide returning to cover the exposed sandbars and mudflats of the coast. But then, when we're just over a spear's throw from the Scots' shield wall, Athelstan raises his hand again and we stamp to a halt.

We still spit out our war chant and quickly we form a ring of shields, so that we stand before the enemy like a living fortress, facing in every direction, defended by our spears which stick out like the spines of a gigantic creature of nightmares.

I stand with Athelstan in the centre of our shield fortress and stare out at the enemy. But strangely nothing happens. Our chanting stops and slowly all of the singing and war cries of all of the armies die away and a silence falls that's filled by the distant murmur of the sea and the cries of the ravens and gulls that still circle above us.

The wind snaps and rattles the many banners and flags, and the white dragon of Wessex, on its field of red, rages against the brilliance of the early morning light.

Then into this pause steps Ara of the Ravens. Her presence seems stronger than it ever has before. She seems almost solid, and as her ravens circle about her, I seem to feel the blast from their powerful wings. Then I realise that this battle has the greatest significance for her. It is here on this field that the country will stand or fall. It is here that the very identity of the land and of those people who live in it will be forged, or smashed apart for ever.

The king stands beneath the dragon's wings of his mighty war banner, and drawing a deep breath he suddenly addresses the armies before him:

"Scots of Alba, Welsh of Strathclyde and Vikings of Dublin: why are you here, standing armed on lands not your own, offering violence to the king to whom you have sworn fealty and service? Why have you broken your given oaths and why do you defile your word and honour before the all-seeing eye of God?

"Blasphemers and oath breakers, put down your weapons and return to the lands from whence you came, cross the seas that carried you here and traverse the borders back to your own God-given kingdoms. Your presence here is neither desired nor is it legal unless I summon you into my presence, and that I have not done.

"Obey now my commands or I will raise sword and spear against you and I will chastise you even unto death."

His voice should have been torn to shreds by the wind, but strangely each word seems to be seized and somehow cast far and wide over the enemy, so that more hear his speech than normally would or should have been able to. Many of them don't understand him, but the reaction of those who do has the effect he wants, and after a moment of perfect silence a great roar of anger and hatred erupts from the enemy and the sky is filled with a great bellow that echoes over the land.

Athelstan smiles at me. "Well, that's done the trick. We seem to have their undivided attention. Now all we have to do is keep them occupied for a few hours."

I watch as the line of Scots before us suddenly billows like a sail in a strengthening wind and then bursts forward and rages down on us, charging over the land, screeching and howling as it comes. And the Scots don't come alone, but bring their Danish and Welsh friends with them.

I stand in the centre of our ring of shields with Athelstan and his war band and also with his unit of javelin throwers that he's holding in reserve. Our ring of shields is enormous and encloses a wide sweep of land with soldiers standing ten ranks deep from the outer to the inner edge, but even so it's dwarfed by the great ocean of warriors that now swarms around us. Soon we're completely surrounded.

As I watch, I wonder how I'm going to survive more than a few minutes in the face of this onslaught. How long can the shield wall stand before it's stoved in by the massive weight of the armies around it? But then I remember, this is the army of Wessex, the force that under the command of the Saxon King Alfred was the first to defeat the Danish Great Army that had smashed its way through Europe before landing on our shores. This is the army that under the command of King Edward and Aethelflaed, the Lady of the Mercians, took back the lands that had been conquered by the Vikings and made the Danes that lived there accept Saxon rule. And it was this army too that made one kingdom from many, a kingdom that we now call England, under the rule of my master, King Athelstan.

I send up a prayer for deliverance and watch as with a mighty, crashing roar the enemy drives into our shields, forcing our soldiers back, but then I watch as this army of Wessex, with a great heave that sends ripples through the ranks, pushes back the Scots, the Welsh and the Danes and defiantly redresses their line.

I'm afraid, in fact I'm very afraid – who on this earth wouldn't be when facing the possibility, even the *probability*, of death? But fear isn't the greatest feeling that fills me as I watch the battle begin. Greatest of all is a strange excitement that almost every warrior can feel when a battle begins. I feel strong, and able to take lives with ease. Is this wrong? Nobody has ever told me that it is, especially for a soldier, and yet for a moment I feel a doubt nagging at the edge of my mind.

But I haven't time to worry about any of this. We're fighting for our survival as a country and as a people. A great roar rises up and I watch as the royal war banner of the Scots rolls forward and I know Constantine their king is joining the fight. I see him clearly, a tall man with grey in his beard and beside him a younger man who can only be his grown son.

With a piercing scream the Scottish king leads his soldiers in a charge that smashes into our shields and drives them back. I look at Athelstan, expecting him to lead us into the struggle, but he shakes his head and I turn back to watch our line repulse the Scots again. Neither side asks for mercy, and warriors fall on both sides. I watch as comrade steps forward over fallen comrade to take his place in the wall of shields.

The roar and clamour of the fighting rises into the air, making the battle song that every warrior knows. The enemy swirls around our living fortress and breaks against us again and again. Now the scent of blood and worse joins with the salt of the sea to fill my nostrils. And the screams of the wounded and dying drown out the cries of the ravens and gulls that keep swooping low, looking for a chance to begin their feasting.

The sun steadily climbs the sky as the day wears on, and still we fight. The enemy's numbers seem endless and yet their corpses pile up around our position, and our own dead are dragged from the wall and laid out in the centre of our fortress. How long can we fight on? Our soldiers are breathing heavily and already seem exhausted. I look beyond our shields to where rank on rank of the Danes wait for their turn to hack at our position, and I see their raven banner suddenly rise higher as though its bearer is preparing to advance. I tug Athelstan's sleeve and point to the banner and, as we both watch, the Vikings form into a spearhead of shields: a wedge shape bristling with spears, swords and axes. As one they rise up on their toes and charge.

The king immediately draws his sword and barks an order. His war band raise their shields and we watch as the Danes hit our wall, the wedge shape of their formation forcing apart the shields and driving deep through the ranks.

Athelstan leaps forward and we follow. But strangely he leaves his javelin throwers in reserve.

We cross the wide 'O' of the space enclosed by our wall at a dead run. We can see the Viking wedge still driving through our ranks. If they breach our wall everything will be lost.

We hit them like a massive hammer and stop them dead as the crack of shield against shield rises up into the air like a thunderclap. I'm still with Athelstan protecting his flank. All is chaos and I hack down a Dane as he raises his spear to kill my king. Athelstan strikes again and again and none can stand against him.

He draws a mighty breath. "TO ME! TO ME, SOLDIERS OF WESSEX! DRIVE THEM BACK! DRIVE THEM BACK!"

Back comes the roar: "THE KING! THE KING! STAND WITH THE KING!" and the fyrd and the housecarles form around us, healing the breach and forcing the enemy back. But now the Scots and Welsh join with their allies and the roar rises to a crescendo. A raging face, mouth open, fills my vision and I thrust my sword between its teeth until blood cascades over the blade. I pull it back and the face sinks from view. Now another warrior strikes at me with his spear. I catch it on my shield and twist to the side so the warrior stumbles forward, his arm over-reaching and exposing his neck. I hack down at the place where neck joins shoulder and blood cascades in a fountain.

But more and more of the enemy rush to the point where the King of the English fights and our wall begins to buckle again. I lose count of how many I fell. My arm aches and my breath rattles in my throat.

"HOLD THEM, SOLDIERS OF WESSEX, HOLD THEM!" Athelstan roars and our warriors dig their feet into the earth and push back as their swords, spears and axes rain down on the enemy ranks. The enemy now rallies around the Scottish king and drives forward again. Athelstan advances to meet them and I'm with him as he strikes down the warrior holding the banner of the Scots. I leap forward, trying to seize the flag, and king and war band join me in the struggle to take the trophy, but the Scots are brave and fierce fighters and surge forward, take up the flag and stand against us toe to toe. Soon we're fighting our own small war within the battle as we struggle to take the prize. But no matter how hard we try, we can't seize it; the Scots are afire with fighting rage and Athelstan draws us back, but not before he has saluted their valour, holding the hilt of his sword to his brow and bowing. For a moment the enemy warriors frowningly nod in acknowledgement as they secure their banner and withdraw in their turn.

Now our line is slowly redressed and our shields finally close over the breach. Athelstan stays in the wall until he's sure all is secure as a line in battle can be and then he leads his war band back to the centre of our living fortress. His javelin throwers still wait to enter the battle and I watch as one of their number presents himself to the king and asks permission to join the struggle, but Athelstan shakes his head and orders them to wait.

From where I stand in the centre of our ring of shields I watch as the struggle grinds on. The enemy swirls around us like a howling gale. Enemy voices mingle into a great formless roar while our soldiers spit out our war chant:

"*OUT!* OUT! OUT! *OUT!* OUT! OUT! *OUT!* OUT! OUT!"

But now there's a shift: the mood and the *feel* of the day change. I watch as the enemy draws back and we're left like a rock at high tide, exposed and torn and damaged. But even so we still stand and we're still unbreached. For a moment silence falls, apart from the call of the ravens and gulls, and I wait holding my breath, knowing that something must happen. I feel... in fact, I *know* that this is the point when everything will change. Again, I feel Ara and her ravens standing with me. Her face is set into a rictus of determination. This shield wall *will* stand; this country *will* survive.

A lone voice from the ranks of the enemy rises up, calling something in the language of the Welsh, and then another joins it from the Scots and a third from the Danes. And then with a great crash the entire combined armies of those who hate us give a great roar as though all the wolves of the world have joined together and are howling for our blood.

Athelstan raps out an order and his javelin throwers snap to attention and raise their spears. Behind them stands a collection of barrels and every one of them is packed with the light throwing-spears they've been training with throughout our entire march north and even before. It seems the king thinks the time to use them has come, and each of the soldiers takes three javelins and walks to a point several paces from the inner edge of the shield wall. None of them carries a shield and each wears only a steel cap, light tunic and leggings. Speed is one of their major weapons, and I hope deadly accuracy is too.

The howling of the enemy continues on and on as they whip themselves into a frenzy. Now the strength of our wall will be tested to its limits; now we either stand or we die.

The howling rises and rises then suddenly changes pitch and the enemy charges, a great rolling wave of hatred smashing down towards us. I watch as it hits and the shield wall is pushed back as our soldiers fall before the onslaught. Athelstan shouts an order and the front row of javelin throwers leap forward in a wild run, but just before they crash into the rear of our wall they throw their spears. The weapons streak through the air as straight as striking falcons and hit the enemy over the rims of their shields. Countless numbers fall, eyes, and throats pierced by the razor-sharp spearheads, and then the second row run in and throw their javelins. Once more enemy soldiers fall like wheat before the scythe, as another line of throwers run forward and cast their spears. The line gradually straightens as our soldiers push back against the charge and the throwers continue to rain down death on the enemy.

Athelstan now draws his sword, and choosing a point where the wall seems most threatened he leads his war band in a charge. Once more I find myself in a chaos of screaming warriors. Our spears and swords thrust and hack at them, but still they push forward, bringing down our soldiers and pushing us back. Soon we're being forced in towards the centre of our own ring of shields. There are just too many of them. We can't hold them for much longer!

But I see the javelin throwers still holding their own line and bringing down countless numbers of Danes and Scots and Welsh. Even so, the onslaught continues. More and more of the enemy charge against us. Some I'm sure must've come from the rear of their army and are fresh to the fighting. Where are the Mercians? Where are the Mercians? If they don't come soon we'll all be slaughtered.

I can hardly feel my arm as I chop and hack at the warriors before me; my breath rattles in my throat and my chest burns. I can't go on for much longer. But then a strange quiet settles on the air, the wind drops and even the ravens and gulls stop calling. It's almost as though someone has closed a huge door on the raging racket of the battle, and I can even hear the distant sea crashing against the shore.

I look up and I see that the king also stands quietly, his head on one side and his hand raised as though asking for silence. Then I hear it. A single horn sounds on the air, tiny and distant, but it's sounding a charge. And I know, somehow I just know that it's the call of the Mercians.

Athelstan throws back his head and laughs. "THE MERCIANS! THE MERCIANS ARE HERE!" he bellows and a great cheer rises up from our hard-pressed warriors and flows around and around our wall of shields, so that the air is filled with our joy.

Now we strike back at our enemies with new energy and power, and they look about them nervously and take a step back. Then a distant roar of onset echoes over the sky and we know that the Mercians are attacking the enemy flanks.

The huge army before us seems to writhe like a great animal in agony. Fear and pure panic can be seen in the men's faces. For a moment the Scottish king and his son rally their fighters and they begin to push forward again, but then with the speed of a striking snake a javelin buries itself in the neck of the young Scottish prince and he falls into his father's arms. I watch as the old warrior breaks the shaft of the javelin in his bare hands and then cradles his dead son to his chest, his face a mask of grief and despair, then his war band surrounds him and they carry the body of their prince away and drag their king after.

The Danes are already in retreat, I know many of their greatest leaders have fallen during the day and they can't face any more killing. The horns of the Mercians sound again and again, drawing closer and closer as they push back the enemy.

Athelstan now raises his sword and roars out a great wordless shout. I charge with his war band, hitting the ranks of the enemy before us. We drive forward, pushing them back and killing as we go. Then at last, a great cry of despair rises up from those who've tried to destroy us, and they turn and run. They turn and run, leaving their hopes in ruins, leaving Athelstan still King of the English, leaving Athelstan still the paramount ruler of all Britain!

And then at this moment of victory I see Ara and her ravens again. And I finally understand her role in all these happenings. I know that she is here to see this moment when the new nation of England, made from the old kingdoms of this land, proves it is strong enough to survive for as long as there are those willing to defend it.

Her ravens add their voices to the great roar of triumph that echoes over the land.

XVII

I'm not proud of what we did. I'm not proud of the way we chased the enemy down to the sea, hacking down warriors who just wanted to get away and live. I'm not proud of the way we chased the Danes and the Scots and the Strathclyde Welsh into the waves where many of them drowned, trampled under the feet of their comrades as they struggled to climb aboard the boats that would take them to safety. I'm not proud of the fact that we killed fighters who'd thrown away their shields and weapons in an effort to get away faster from our swords and axes. And neither, I think, was Athelstan, because as soon as he could, he called in his army and we watched as the Danish dragon boats unfurled their sails and headed out to sea. I thought I saw the Scottish king sitting in the stern of one of the ships with the body of his son cradled in his lap. But I can't be sure; it could've been any one of the thousands of warriors who'd seen someone they loved die in the fighting.

It's now Christmas and the court is celebrating at the royal palace in Chippenham in Wessex. Athelstan uses these times to call the other kings to his court to act as witnesses to important new laws that have been made. The Danes come from East Anglia, the Welsh from Cymru and Constantine is called from Scotland.

The celebrations have been going on for days and I think the court has drunk enough beer, wine and mead to float a ship. But Christmas is also a time for business and I stand behind Athelstan's chair in the Council Chamber as he waits to greet the other kings of the islands. The chamber is almost as big as the Mead Hall, and the floor is flagged with tiles and wide slabs of stone.

The place is packed with councillors, scribes and advisors and the noise almost equals the sound of the celebrations. But now the guards at the huge double doors of the chamber thump their spear shafts on the stone floor slowly, three times to announce important arrivals.

The noise in the chamber dies away and we watch as a strange procession makes its way across the floor. Before us walks a line of men, shoulder to shoulder like a shield wall without the shields. These are the kings summoned by Athelstan, as paramount ruler of these islands, to bear witness to the law codes that he has pronounced. None wants to appear less important than their fellow kings, so none may go forward in front of another, and because of this they have to walk in a line abreast to underline their equality.

Athelstan stands to receive them and watches with a face that reveals nothing of his feelings. My own I know is different, and if any of the kings could be bothered to look at a lowly servant such as me, they'd see the hatred I feel for each and every one of them; they'd see the grief I feel for the deaths of so many in that greatest of battles, and they'd see the contempt I feel for how ridiculous they look as they struggle to keep in exact step with each other.

The Welsh from Cymru seem the most relaxed; they may not have answered our call to arms but at least they didn't fight against us. And the Danes swagger as they always swagger, almost as though they'd never been defeated and made to accept peace. Only Constantine, the king of the Scots, seems different. He walks like a man who knows his people will always fight with power and might against any who come against them. A man of pride, with good reason to be proud.

They finally stop before Athelstan and I watch as he spreads wide his arms. "Welcome, my fellow kings of these islands. You alone of all who dwell under these skies have the majesty and power that permits you to bear witness to the making of laws, that most important of monarchical acts. Let us begin then the process that makes order out of chaos and good government from the rule of the mob."

He steps down from the dais where his chair stands and I watch as he singles out Constantine by taking his hand and nodding his head in kingly greeting, one ruler to another. "I too lost family in that battle," I hear him say quietly. "Two cousins, not the same as a son, blood of your blood, flesh of your flesh, but family just the same. Perhaps we have a bond in that grief, Constantine. Perhaps all of us who fought there have this bond."

The old Scottish warrior holds his gaze, his eyes narrowed, but eventually he nods in return, though I have to stare hard to see it as his head barely moves.

The vellum scrolls on which the laws are written are then brought out and the long process and ceremony of witnessing begins.

Later that night I stand in the small courtyard attached to Athelstan's private quarters. Rumble-stump is with me and I watch as he follows a scent, snuffling loudly. It's a crystal-clear night and the stars glitter brilliantly in that deepest blue that isn't quite black.

I'm tired and ready for bed, but I remember Athelstan's words when I spoke to him about King Constantine after the ceremony.

"Does he feel friendship for me? Well no, of course not! He hates me, as he has every right to. His son died in that battle and he blames me for that. Why should he feel anything for me but the most powerful sort of loathing?"

"He took your hand and nodded in greeting."

"To be exact, I took his hand and if he did nod his head, not many were able to see it. No, he hates me, which is fair enough. But at least we both now know that we can work together again… at least for a while."

Now Rumblestump comes bumbling up, begging for a fuss, and I ruffle his ears and stand looking at the stars again. I can feel the presence of Ara of the Ravens, but I don't search the shadows to find her. Now that the kingdom is safe for a while, perhaps she'll rest and let others defend its borders.

I'm just taking a deep breath and thinking of the new year that's approaching fast, and all that may happen in the coming months, when the king's voice calling from the doorway suddenly interrupts my thoughts.

"What are you doing, Edwin – it's freezing. Come in and shut the door! And bring that under-sized excuse for a dog with you – he can lie by the fire while I warm my feet on him."

I ruffle Rumblestump's ears again and then we both go inside and I shut the door on the cold.

Historical Note

The dating of events in Anglo-Saxon history can be difficult. Often the sources don't bother with exact dates, but those used here are generally accepted as accurate.

Athelstan was crowned King of the Saxons in 925 AD but he didn't become 'King of the English' and so ruler of all the people and land of England until 927 AD, after he had taken control of York from its Viking rulers. Like all the Saxon monarchs of this period, he seems to have spent much of his time fighting wars and trying to strengthen his position.

The Battle of Brunanburh in 937 AD was his greatest victory and it was from this point on that the boundaries of England, Scotland and Wales that we know today were more or less established. But only two years later, in October 939 AD, Athelstan died. He had never married and was succeeded as king by his half-brother Edmund.

Directly after Athelstan's death, York chose a new Viking king and it wasn't until 954 AD that the Saxon King Eadred (Edmund's brother) regained control of York and Northumbria and finally re-established the boundaries of England that Athelstan had made.

Athelstan was a great soldier and politician who made the land that we know today as England. And it was because of him that the borders of all the countries on this island we call Britain were drawn and still remain.

Bonus Bits!

Guess who

Each piece of information below is about one of the characters in the story. Match the character to the information, and then check your answers at the end of this section. No peeking!

1 Edwin's Mum
2 Athelstan's first dog
3 brother of Lady Aethelflaed
4 shoemaker
5 has red hair and green eyes
6 has blond hair and blue eyes
7 daughter of Alfred the Great
8 ill and confined to bed before he died

A Edwin
B Edmund
C Cwen
D Lord Ethelred
E Athelstan
F Lady Aethelflaed
G Bumble
H King Edward of Wessex

Whose flag?

Each of the armies marches under a different flag. Can you match up the correct army to the correct flag? The answers are at the end of the book.

Black raven	Mercia
White dragon	Danes
Yellow wyvern	Wessex

What was the Battle of Tettenhall?

We know about this battle from a document called the Anglo-Saxon Chronicle. The battle was said to have taken place on 5th August in the year 910. It has also been called the Battle of Wednesfield. The forces of Mercia and Wessex were allies and met an army of Northumbrian Vikings in Mercia.

We don't know a lot about the actual battle but it is clear that the allies trapped the Vikings and inflicted very heavy casualties on them. The Anglo-Saxon Chronicle reports that many thousands of Vikings were killed, as well as their kings.

Quiz time

How much can you remember about he story? Look back at the book to find the answers if you need to.

1. Who does Edwin punch near the beginning of the story?
   A Edmund
   B The Prince of Wessex
   C Master Goodwin
   D Lord Ethelred

2. What is the name of the armed force every man between 14 and 60 takes part in?
   A fyrd
   B shield
   C Thurlbear
   D army

3. Who is Edwin's family ghost?
   A his mum
   B his grandmother
   C his great aunt
   D his great grandmother

4. What is put in Edwin's helmet on his first day of training?
   A axle grease
   B oil
   C cow dung
   D pig dung

5. Who made Southampton into a fortified town?

   A Lord Ethelred

   B The Prince of Wessex

   C King Alfred

   D Lady Aethelflaed

6. Where are the Kings of Wessex anointed?

   A Chelmsford

   B London

   C Winchester

   D Kingston-upon-Thames

What Next?

If you enjoyed reading this story why not look for some non-fiction books about the same period of history? Can you find out more facts about Athelstan?

Have a think about these questions after reading this story:

Why do you think Edwin and Athlestan got on so well together?

Athlestan says in the story, "If you're going to lie, do it with confidence, that way everyone will believe you". What do you think about this saying? Discuss with friends whether lying is ever ok.

Answers to "Guess Who"
1C, 2G, 3H, 4B, 5A, 6E, 7F, 8D

Answers to "Whose Flag"
Black raven = Danes
White dragon = Wessex
Yellow Wyvern = Mercia

Answers to "Quiz Time"
1B, 2A, 3C, 4D, 5C, 6D